DIGGING UP THE BONES
Dale Marlowe

DIGGING UP THE BONES
Dale Marlowe

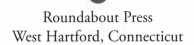

Roundabout Press
West Hartford, Connecticut

www.roundaboutpress.com

LCCN: 2014942370
ISBN: 978-0-98-588124-5

Text set in Adobe Garamond
Cover and text design by Sara Lewis
Cover images and art by Jeff Williams
Author photo courtesy of Dale Marlowe
Printed in the United States of America

FIRST EDITION

9 8 7 6 5 4 3 2 1

To Amy

Digging Up The Bones

PATERNOSTER

EBB HOLLER 1997

The undertaker and the preacher frown, nod, pat our arms
and backs, but check their watches when they think we're not
looking. Distant relatives come blue-haired, shuffling, roused
by rumors or a chance reading of the Old Man's obituary in
the *Slocum County Register*. I don't know why they cry. Maybe
the luxury of kinship without proximity allows them to
remember him as they wish he'd been, instead of how he was.
They're old too, and his passing invokes the inevitability of
theirs. Perhaps they weep for themselves, or because the rest
of us will not.

Raindrops burst on the tarp overhead. Vapor shrouds the
obelisks and rain-slick headstones. The peaks above seem
neutered, cut down, rounded smooth by a hundred thousand
years of wind, water, and fire. A pair of hounds bay nearby, and
a coal train winds through the holler. The Old Man was a miner;
it's fitting a locomotive's moan would be his dirge. He'll go to
ground to the pounding tune of a train on a slow crawl loaded
with obsidian dunes, going wherever it is they take the coal.

I stand across from my mother and father, the casket between. Even in death, the Old Man splits us. My mother presses her hand against the small of my father's back. She stares up into his tawny whittled face, its color owed to some race other than the Scots we claim. Jaw set, teeth clenched, neck wet with frustration. He's uncomfortable in a tie. If he squeezes his fists any tighter, they'll implode.

Aunt Tonya grips her husband's elbow. He's much older, but they say he treats her right. She leans hard on her daughter Sherry's shoulder. Her face is an old woman's: skin taut over her skull, eyes deep in purple-rimmed sockets. She lives in shadow, drawing more light than she reflects.

My uncles, Wayne and Cory, stand beside me in the same plaid flannel dyed different shitty Wal-Mart shades; Cory's, blue and green, Wayne's, red and yellow. Wayne's looks like our McKean tartan: a thin yellow cross under four black horizontal bands on a field of burgundy. Both smoke Camel Wides, unfiltered, lighting the next with the current. Cory reeks of cheap drugstore cologne.

The young preacher sports a whisk broom copstache. His mixed accent betrays an education beyond the hills. My cousins think he's wise, but they mistake condescension for wisdom. Swollen with apocalyptic surety, he uses what he imagines to be the vocabulary of first-century Palestine: "Here lies a man perfected, his spirit taken to the bosom of Almighty God. He's there, saints. I'm sure of it. I spent time with the Nash family! I saw a miracle! A sweet granddaughter pray her papaw to the Lord, Amen."

He means cousin Sherry, who rocks back and forth, fingers over her mouth and nose. She's one of the few born outside the Old Man's reddest years, and came on him sick and plaintive, looking for a redemption no one else would give. She bathed him, kept him company, wiped his ass. She doesn't know why we can't forgive. She has not heard, won't hear, won't learn. The rest are long gone, anyway—too bitter of mind, too removed in place to care. They fled because these hills smell of him: like sour mash, coal dust, and blood.

I have thought about this. I have decided not to hold it against her.

She shows no trace of the habits that vex us. Neither booze nor drugs tempt her. She's nonviolent, monogamous, noncriminal, and polite. A young mother at eighteen, but married first. I envy that life, centered on husband and child, but I pity her, too. Her life is complete before it has begun. With years ahead, and Nash genes within, I hope she can hold steady. Her husband is working up in Dell County. I never met him, but they say he's a good man.

"I can't sugarcoat it," the preacher whinnies. "Errol, Sr. had a wicked streak. But we can learn from his life. That's how he'd want it. O yes, children, the wages of sin is death, Romans 6:23. That's our only birthright, saints. It comes at a time appointed by God. Woe, were it not for Calvary! In Calvary, there's hope!"

This is what some want to hear. They decided the Old Man got saved, which absolves him of his crimes and requires reworking of family legend. Stories will hence be told under disclaimer: *That was before he got saved.* If the Lord has forgiven Errol Nash, Sr., He is not a God the rest of us are prepared to serve.

A fat kid with a red crew cut, and eyes narrowed at the edges by epithelial folds, stands near my cousin Kyle. I don't know him, but he fits among this crew so well I hadn't noticed him until now.

"Yes," he mutters. "O, yes, Jesus, Jesus. Thank You, Jesus."

The preacher slaps the black lambskin covering his ragged Bible. He raises his right hand like he's taking an oath. "Errol,

Sr. made a decision for the Lord—late—but he made it in time. I prayed with him with Sister Sherry, the night the Lord took him home, Amen. All the good this man could've done had he decided for Jesus before that late hour! How great would be his crown in Glory!"

The undertaker, Mr. Giatelli, pushes his brown fedora down. Our family has been good to the Giatellis. Three other Nash graves lie near the Old Man's. A wife, to madness; two sons, murdered: one by fire, the other by electricity.

"O that Errol could speak with us now! He would say tarry not, children, on that road to iniquity! Turn to Jesus, for you know neither the hour nor the day, and He comes as a thief in the night. First Thessalonians 5:2, Amen. What will He say? Will He say 'Welcome, my good and faithful servant,' or will He spit you out, saying 'Depart from me, for I never knew ye'? Matthew 7, Amen. We know Errol, Sr. turned from wickedness, but children, what of you? The sins of the fathers are visited unto the seventh generation, but the grace of Christ can break your bonds! He has bought you out of bondage! Paid your price—won't you turn to the Lord? If you've not accepted Jesus Christ as your Lord and personal Savior, I invite you to come, come."

Even this peacock of a preacher knows when it's time to quit. His altar call is misguided. If he's spent as much time with our family as he claims, he knows who's interested in Jesus and who isn't. If they haven't declared by now, they never will.

"Let us close with the Lord's Prayer," the preacher cries.

The pages of his Bible flutter like shuffling cards. He stops them with his thumb, licks his forefinger, uses the wet tip for traction. We join:

who art in heaven, hallowed be Thy name. Thy kingdom come, Thy will be done, on earth, as it is in heaven. Give us this day

The tarp unfastens, shakes loose. After a short flight, it catches on a tall headstone.

our daily bread. Forgive us our trespasses as we forgive those who trespass against us. Lead us not into temptation, but deliver us from Evil.

Mr. Giatelli's sons sprint from the hearse, lugging thick yellow ropes. Their expressions are varnished solemn, demure but insincere. Feigning grief is as natural to them as a good morning greeting. I have thought about this. I have decided not to hold it against them.

for Thine is the kingdom, the honor, and the glory. Forever, and ever, Amen.

The preacher blesses us. My kin break, each faction drifting toward its cars. Kyle slinks off with the red-haired kid. Water splatters under boots, children chatter, tires hiss and grumble on gravel and wet asphalt. Clouds race across the sky, cloaking the sun well enough to fool the halogen floodlights' sensors. They snap to life, crisp and white, so bright you can hear them.

Tonya looks like a wading heron that lost the shore. Her white miniskirt, carefully pressed and bleached, has a splotch of mud on the hem. She frowns and curses, and her husband helps her as best he can. They say he looks like the Old Man, and I guess he does.

My mother asks my father if he's okay, and when he says he is, she leaves, purse tight under her arm, tiptoeing to the car, shoulders back, suddenly liberated. She's never known how to act around the Nashes; usually chatty, she falls quiet among them. She fears more than she judges, and I don't blame her. I get them, I think. But when we've assembled, the heft of it, the weight of our testimony, clips my tongue, too.

Mr. Giatelli apologizes that he's shorthanded and asks us to help him and the boys lower the coffin. Wayne and Cory remain, but their real reason for staying is to make sure the Old Man gets buried right and doesn't claw his way out. Sherry stays, too. She can't believe the Old Man's gone. The preacher sidles up, his arm winding around her shoulder. "He's in a better place, darlin'." I decide I do not like this preacher. Mr. Giatelli hops around, agitated, worried the uncovered grave is letting too much water into the vault. "Hurry, y'all!" he calls. "Get him in, nice and easy before water collects!"

The Giatelli boys push three ropes beneath the casket and bring the ends across to the other side, making a cradle by which we can lower the Old Man. I grab my end. My father does the same. We pull the rope. When Mr. Giatelli gives the word, we lift. Mr. Giatelli jerks the Astroturf cover from beneath like a novice magician, then squats to remove a piece of plywood as long as the grave and half as wide.

The Old Man was 115 pounds at death, and the casket can't weigh over 150. Six grown men should be able to lift 265 pounds. Still, it's only right we struggle. This coffin holds more than bones—it's dense and laden, a basket of curses. Mr. Giatelli kneels, soiling his trousers' knees. He peers into the vault, hands in the air, like somebody's got a gun between his shoulder blades. Lighting scores the sky behind him.

"Easy boys, easy now. Let her down slow."

We lower the ropes, hand under hand. Thunderclap. My uncles let the rope slack, huffing. Sherry tucks into the preacher's chest. He holds her, whispering, "Jesus, yes, Jesus."

The casket bottom hits the vault floor; echo: water disturbed. Mr. Giatelli says, "Don't worry. Water down there'll evaporate. Casket's watertight—no worries. Oh yeah. That's good. Real good. Pull them ropes."

My father releases. I pull; Cory releases, Wayne pulls. Mr. Giatelli's sons do the same. I'm proud to have helped put the

Old Man down. The Giatellis coil the ropes around their elbows and fists. I hand them mine, but Wayne asks to keep his. Mr. Giatelli chuckles and shrugs, but I don't think he gets it.

Wayne's been a corpse for years, animated by rage, narcotics, and self-pity. With the Old Man gone, he frets he'll forget and one morning soon, he'll wake up thirty-eight, unmarried, unemployed, and illiterate, junked on oxys, and the Old Man will be gone, and none of it made a bit of difference. There'll still be child-support payments, monkeys-on-backs, closed mines, little messes everywhere. It'll be too much to bear, so he wants the rope around to keep the blame sharp and present. If Wayne doesn't dignify his sufferings by nursing them, the Old Man's guilt will fade with passing days.

I'm not one to push closure, whatever that is, if I even believed in pop-psych bullshit, and I don't. But if you need to hate somebody to get up in the morning, you should.

A line of cars forms down on the entrance to KY 38. Taillights, wooden bumpers, sheet plastic on one car's rear window. Tonya waits for Sherry, back on the road near the grave, in the passenger seat of a '68 Ford pickup. Tonya's husband's armpit conceals half her face. My mother waits in our rental.

My father lurks behind the grave. He rubs his nose, then bends at the waist, leans over the grave, and drops a fat, gooey wad of sputum-thick spit. It unrolls at the casket, and his face brightens in a sincere blend of relief and joy so macabre and black-sun bright I can't look at it full on.

I turn my head; when I look back, his face has its normal mien—awkward, aloof, alone. The others saw too, but they ignore it. Wayne and Cory would never say anything. *Errol Junior made it out, did it right, didn't let the Old Man get him.* I know better, but so long as they want to think that, I don't figure anyone should tell them different. If we didn't lie to ourselves, I swear we'd never make it through the day.

Mr. Giatelli points at the plywood and the open pit, gestures wildly, and fusses some more. I shake my head. Four generations in Appalachia, and they still act Italian. "Get the lid on it right-now-in-a-minute boys, just soon as we get these tent poles down and the crane over here." His sons grab the plywood by the sides and put it over the grave.

The preacher has his hand up and his eyes squeezed tight. He sweeps his arm roundhouse, bringing his hand to a stop, pointing, like he's trying to get us to look into the distance. "O Lord, O Jesus," he wails, "we come before Thy throne, Lord…"

Cory frowns. "You want a cigarette?"

"Don't smoke."

He lights up and takes a drag. "Remember when I used to babysit you? You were a little shit. You know that?"

Change of subject: "Staying busy?"

Wayne answers in a tiny voice. "Ginseng. It's up to four hundred dollars a pound. Sell it up in Breathitt. You? Still on that longhaired piece?"

"I'll be in the car," my father mutters, unimpressed with the topic. He starts up the hill.

I mutter something about gentlemen's secrets. Wayne grins around his cigarette and thumps Cory on the arm, and they bray like hyenas. I tell them about Hank, my son, the one thing in this world I'm proud of, the product of my one sincere attempt to settle, the only person besides my mother I ever truly loved. They tell me to make sure Hank knows about Kentucky, his uncles, and the hills.

"Don't worry," I explain. "Kentucky ain't home for Hank, but it's where he comes from."

They ask when I'll be back, how many years it'll be before they see me again, and why somebody has to die before I make it down, analyzing my urban affect, picking me apart like a stolen car, only half kidding. I'm an object of amusement, to be discussed in third person.

"All right, now. Get on home, now, before we get a mind to whip you."

I turn and catch the preacher's visage, illuminated in a joist of sunlight streaming through a cloud break that beatifies him, if only for a second. "Keep Sherry near, Lord, hold her in Your nail-scarred hands as she grieves." Sherry touches my sleeve when I walk past. "God bless your family," coos the preacher. I tell him there's a first time for everything.

We're almost onto KY 38, when outside the rear window I see Sherry and the preacher at the pickup's passenger window, talking to Tonya. Sherry doesn't get in the pickup; instead, she walks with the preacher toward his car.

Cory and Wayne haunt the gravesite, watching Mr. Giatelli swing the arm of a Komatsu halftrack over the hole. The vault lid dangles from the end, precarious, but Mr. Giatelli's sons slouch, bored, beneath it, waiting to guide the lid down and fasten it to the lips of the sarcophagus. Wayne holds the rope, recoiled. A length of it trails behind, and about a quarter remains looped through his fist in an oval, like a hangman's knot. I press my hand to the window.

My father hums. It's only a matter of time before he breaks. I don't know what he'll produce, but it will be loud and long and overdue. It won't be sorrow. I don't think his battered heart can grieve that old fucker. Can you grieve for someone you hate? Sometimes hate feels a lot like love, and it's not nice to say, but there's only a degree of difference between caressing a face and slapping it blue.

The night we got the call the Old Man had died, my father got desperately drunk on Jim Beam, shot after shot after gum-numbing shot. He told me terrible things that caused my stomach to wretch, my veins to thrum, and my breath to burst from my mouth and lungs like I'd been kicked in the chest.

I know what we buried today. As we lowered him, I recited his crimes in my head. Each time I wove one hand under the other, I pretended those eight inches were tiny revenge for those whose lives go lashed daily with echoes of things said and done before they were born, for the proffered ghosts in his seed haunting we who call him our father, and hate him from righteousness and rage, because he was foul, pathetic, and irredeemable, but also from a sense of secret, painful empathy.

In our darkest, lowest, sickest nights we have looked in cracked mirrors and seen his face grinning back at us. It's his mouth that wants strong drink, his lungs that demand strange drugs, his lusts sending us unclothed to places we would not go, his greed pushing us to reach with trembling fingers for things we do not deserve, his cunning that spews lies from our mouths, and his fear that causes our fingers to fold into heavy fists. Yes, I know what we buried.

I have thought about this. I have decided I will hold it against him, forever.

White Folks Just Ain't Made For This heat

Toledo 1985

Errol Nash, Jr. stands before a rack of mortar shells and a pine green semi. He's very thin, and smokes a cigarette. He wears the same black-framed U.S. Army spectacles he wears today. Under his arm, grinning with a platoon of crisp, white teeth, stands the blackest man I've ever seen. He's so dark he looks purple, head shining, bald as a grape. Both lock their fingers on a pinch of air. My father projects his left, the other his right. The gap between my father's thumb and forefinger is two inches. The black man holds half an inch.

I know this code. I've seen it in other Vietnam photos. It means, this is how much longer I have in this shithole. An inch for a year. Closer the fingers, wider the smile.

They wear identical fatigues. My father is shirtless. He holds a Hamm's beer can, tilted thirty degrees—no spills; the can is empty, or near it, and he's drunk, mugging like Vietnam's a party. You can see affection in the posture, of two bodies pulled close, as if gravity itself draws them in. They grip like brothers; as though without one, the other could not stand. That was another time.

Today I counted, and my father has said *nigger* eighteen times.

I tuck the photo in my breast pocket and crawl backward to the attic floor's opening and down into the garage. I fold the stairs into the attic door, then raise it into the ceiling. I feel a stare on my neck. My father stands behind me, weight on his good leg, sucking a Bud forty-ounce. I turn. He wears a NASCAR cap, a dark blue T-shirt, beige Dickies, and a weekend's stubble. He pushes his glasses up the bridge of his nose. He's got the puss of a pissed off drunk who wants a fight, but can't find a reason to start one.

"Snooping?"

"Looking for mementos," I say. "I'm making a scrapbook for Hank."

"Why the hell a baby need a scrapbook for?"

"For when he's older. Dinner ready?"

"You can't just go taking things."

I take the kitchen doorknob in my palm and reassure him.

"No sweat."

"Don't patronize me."

There it is: the opening salvo in the argument the alcohol demands. But I'm already in the house, where my girlfriend and my mother are locked in a passive-aggressive waltz. Debbie tries to help, but my mother directs her to some lesser task, so Debbie knows her skills as a homemaker have been noted, considered, and found wanting. Peeling the wrappers from Lipton bags, Debbie waits for my mother to turn away, then rolls her eyes.

I can't understand why we live here—a hundred degrees in the summer, no ocean; ten degrees in the winter, no mountains. There's a breeze coming in, but it doesn't lift the humidity. Despite the heat, the kitchen smells how I imagine a farmhouse kitchen would've a hundred years ago: heated brown cane sugar, okra, ham, black coffee, soup beans, black-eyed peas, green beans, chow-chow, and buttered corn.

My father slumps in a chair at the table's end. Darling Hank glides about the cramped kitchen, bumping shins. A shock of red hair the shade of my beard blooms on his forehead. Debbie calls him her Scottish Unicorn. They've put him in a little pair of pink sunglasses. When he's older, I will show his girlfriends pictures of it. I remove the sunglasses and squat next to him.

"Watch it, buster."

"*Nahhh!*"

He scoots off, giggling like a crazy person, flying under the radar of drunk grandpas and rivalries between grannies and babymamas. My mother stirs a cup of milk into an iron skillet, followed by a sprinkling of flour.

"Debbie, honey? Why don't you set the table?"

"Never mind." I say. "I'll—"

Debbie interrupts. "I'd love to."

Suddenly, a burnt odor: "Mother?" I say, "What about—"

Hissing a chain of Baptist half-curses, she flings the oven open, slides her hand into an oven mitt, and plunges her arm into the smoke. A second later, she drops an aluminum cookie sheet on the stove. Biscuits smolder on it in squat piles. Debbie walks by, carrying an armful of plates, face smug. Schadenfreude, evil, entirely justified. I lift Hank from the walker and drop him into his highchair. He revs up the droning cry babies use to punish parents. I lean in and read him my version of the riot act.

"Stop, Hank. No."

When it comes to setting my father's place, Debbie pauses.

She doesn't like to be near him when he's drinking. I don't blame her, but in the past few minutes the breeze seems to have calmed him. He's gone from feisty to drowsy.

She gives his setting the attention and care she gave the three other spaces. Fork, knife. Plate, spoon. Folded napkin. Glass, half-full with ice. She never fails their expectations of politeness, and gives them no ammunition. She bends over him in a way I notice, but they can't.

I am her lover, trained by time and lust in a language for which her body's movements provide the grammar. I will take their punishment later, should any be due. My mother carries a course of bowls and platters to the table, along with a sad, half-crushed loaf of white bread. She untwists the orange tie.

"Reckon we'll eat Wonder bread."

We ignore Hank's crying with strained patience and drop the subject of singed biscuits, fearful we might use the second-person accusative, implying fault, and cause my mother to explain where fault should lie: her antique stove, inferior Bisquick yeast, lack of help around the kitchen. Debbie dumps a heap of mashed potatoes in a red plastic bowl, and presents it to Hank, who promptly plunges his fist deep inside.

"*Nahhh!*"

He's been trying to talk. He pounds his highchair, sometimes my chest, then tears off a syllable like a good burp. My mother thinks his first word will be Nana, and Debbie agrees, but I think they're wrong. I read someplace *no* is the word we hear most over a lifetime, certainly during infancy. By the time a kid's five he's heard *no* about fourteen thousand times. I read that, and first thing I thought was *nahhh*. Then I caught myself and laughed.

My mother offers a grueling grace. There's something pushy about the way Fundies pray around non-believers—at us, for us, but not with us. We're unmarried, with a baby, and every moment before God is a chance for Him—by which one should understand *her*—to show us the way from sin.

She loads my father's plate for him: a thick, pink slab of ham, two spoons of mashed potatoes, green beans, gravy over all, buttered white bread, and a smattering of okra. He sips his beer, accepts the plate.

We eat. The food is lard-laden, good, fattening, and filling, but I can't enjoy it. I'm only half present, listening for pauses or for people to address me, to insert my nods and grunts so as to camouflage my lack of interest. I'm lost in my head, gone twenty years back, lurking among real men, soldiers in Vietnam, a country I will never see.

What I've filched from the attic the past few months isn't worth anything, unless you reckon by nostalgia. Knickknacks from Kentucky, tchotchkes from Hawaii, silver coins, World War II medals, mementos from Korea and Vietnam, somebody's Kiwanis tie tack, some scratched 45s and, of course, every photo I can find.

I wasn't much older than Hank when the photo was snapped. I want to preserve this proof of my father hugging his favorite boogeyman, but just now it disturbs me so much I need to keep it close, get my mind around it, look at it, fiddle with it, turn it over, learn it, solve it like a riddle.

After dinner, it's Tigers versus Indians. I doubt my father can see the game. His glasses scrip is fifteen years old, and so far from correcting his vision he might as well go without. He cradles Hank in the crook of one arm, which leaves his drinking hand free.

"You should see an ophthalmologist."

"Mind your business."

At the next timeout, a commercial plays featuring a white, managerial type—three piece suit, paunch, aloof expression, the whole deal—in a hurry, jogging from an airport gate. The crowd splits, and Reggie Jackson, in full uniform plus Louisville Slugger, calls out. The man hearkens. Jackson tosses up a thick sheaf of paper folded lengthwise, in thirds. Jackson brings his bat around, sending the sheaf to the man in a soft drive. The man snatches the papers from the air. A close-up of the unfolded sheaf reveals a rental car contract and a set of car keys. Overjoyed, the fusty man swings his elbow around like he's about to yell *attaboy*! and bellows, "Thanks, Budget! Just in time!" The camera focuses on Jackson: "Budget executive business service. We go to bat for you."

Fade to black. Next, Sandy Duncan and Triscuits. My father rests his beer on the recliner's side table. He beckons like he's going to lay a big secret on me.

"Old Man said it. He was plumb crazy, but he was right when he said niggers was going to take over. That was back in the fifties. Look! Ain't twelve percent the country and a hundred percent pro-ball and half the TV. Everywhere I look that Cosby's on. Got John Thompson, buck nigger coaches Georgetown, says he won't play a white boy. Breakdancing, that other…damn fool…*pup-pff-putoot*."

Was my father was trying to beat box? Sweet Jesus. "Rap?" I asked.

"That other's name? Jackson?"

"Reggie?"

"Jessie! Fine pimp, got him a bullhorn in one hand, a collection plate in the other, and he'd drop either to squeeze a white woman's titty. Ran for president. Gonna get worse. Niggers."

He says nigger in auditory italics, with a sour hate and a rebel's joy. At first I argued. He'd call me stupid, tell me I'd not spent enough time with them to know how they do, and I'd learn, and soon, dumb as I was. Beers later, he'd accuse me of getting above my raising. Then he'd curse me and call me a nigger lover. There was little hope of convincing him he was wrong. I set logic aside, and offered no reply but silence.

Debbie enters.

"Here," she says, scooping Hank from my father's arm.

She whisks Hank into the kitchen. He starts fussing right off. He's teething. He cut her nipple earlier this week. They're using those sunglasses to distract him—on, clap and laugh; off, where'd they go? On again, clap and laugh. He gives them infrequent *nahhh*s.

In as much a surprise to me as it is to my father, I ask—or, rather the question asked itself: "Who was your friend in the Army?"

"Had a hundred."

"The black guy."

"Huh?"

I place the picture on the ottoman between us.

He pinches the photo's corner, stands, and walks out the front door. I follow. He stands on the walk between the front door and a row of evergreen shrubs. He draws a matchbook from his pocket, strikes, and holds the match to the photo. Orange flames take the sides; ovals singe the middle, melting him and the man in slow motion. Fire licks his fingertips, and he drops the remainder to the cement and grinds the ashes with his boot sole.

"Who was that?"

Nothing.

Frustrated, I start toward the front door, but as I reach for the handle, he speaks.

"I wrote your mama dirty letters. Sex letters. They're in that box. You get them too? Fuckin' thief."

I cross my arms and look away, but he picks up a thread, like he's been telling the story for years.

"First week in country I got laid up heat sick. Passed out on the tarmac, one step off the plane. You know it gets up to a hundred and twenty degrees. Sure does. Terrence—that was him—he lived in our barracks. Brought me *Playboy* magazines while I got right. Says to me, he says, 'Nudie mag ain't hurt you, son. Look at them glasses! Hell, you already blind.' Told the nurse, he says, 'White folk just ain't made for this heat.' He wasn't like them others, didn't think it was their war."

"It wasn't," I say. "Wasn't yours, either."

"One time he tells me, he says, 'Blood here, crackers too. Everybody poor. You don't see no rich boys up'n this motherfucker. Hear? No beef with Charlie. No beef with you. Just trying to get my black ass home.' You don't think about it like that till somebody tells you to. Once you do you can't think about it no other way again.

"One night we come out of Hue toward A Shau, where them boys in the hundred-and-first and the third-of-the-fifths taking it hard at Dong Ap Bia. Hamburger Hill. They made a movie. One them Vietnam movies. You see that?"

"Only one I've seen is *Apocalypse Now*."

He wags his finger in my face.

"Deeper and deeper. Boys die to take a paddy, DC calls saying give it back. Deeper and deeper. Well, that night we led a convoy, pulling a trailer of shells. He drove. Come over the ridge on A Shau. This fucker. That stupid nigger."

The hate in his voice, a straight razor.

"Trying to get to FSB Destiny, right on the shit, but Charlie had buzz saws all the way. Come dark, them roads was Charlie's. Destiny radioed in telling us to wait it out at Birmingham. They ain't but sig-foured and my face is wet, pants sopping wet, looking like Jell-O spilt on the legs. I look over to Terrence and that nigger's slumped over, looking at me, or looks like he's looking at me, top his head clean off. Blowed him away."

His face contorts—but it's not his face, but a snap visage of the foul parasite hollowing him inside out. A moan starts deep in his lungs, and leaves his mouth in a high-volume, prehistoric wail, a painful scream so real and unrefined by language it's less the utterance of a man, more the keening of a trapped beast. He punches the air, wobbling, hand held outward, thumb and forefinger separated an eighth of an inch.

"This goddamn close. This close! Gone, ain't he? I'm left, got that sight in my head. Fuck me, they opened his skull like a can of beans."

He slithers by, hand hiding his eyes, and walks inside. My mother, who'd been sitting in the living room near the picture window, trying to eavesdrop, follows too.

"Junior? Junior?"

He ignores her and marches into the kitchen. She corners me, takes a hands-on-hip pose for demanding an explanation, but she hears him sniffle, and falls silent. Whatever happened to him is beyond her ability to heal. I hear the fridge opening, closing. A twist-top unscrewed.

I retreat to my old double bed, the mattress upon which I lay the first time I beat off, accidentally and gloriously, and then lost my virginity, somewhat less triumphantly. Tonight, Debbie and Hank doze there, blanketed by those memories, and in some way, products of them. I slide in behind her, spoon her, and chase sleep. It eludes me. I pull her close, cup her breast.

"Drama?"

"That's one word for it."

"Junior okay?"

I sound off. "*Negative*, ma'am."

"Your mother wasn't so bad. I'm glad we're leaving tomorrow."

My mother lays a fine breakfast spread. Fried eggs and potatoes, sausage, sausage gravy, biscuits unburnt, fresh coffee, halved grapefruit, buttered toast and jelly. My father sits at the end of the table hurriedly spooning egg into his mouth, loading his fork while he chews. He gulps coffee instead of sipping.

My mother looks at him, then me, then Debbie, then her plate. "Hon, put Hank's sunglasses on him," she says, without looking up.

Debbie retrieves them from the counter and hangs them on his nose.

"How cute!" my mother squeals.

Hank leans forward, doing the *nahh-nahh* dance. He puffs his cheeks. Hank puckers, wiggling, beating his fat little baby arms on the white plastic tray of his highchair. Full to the teeth, he blows.

"*Nig-uh!*"

He raises his arms and cheers, expecting cheers. My heart sags. My mother: "Lord, did Hank just say—?"

My father's eyes open so wide in this protracted instant they reveal his core—cold and empty and cruel and manic and helpless. Debbie gasps. She drops her fork on the table.

"Hank? Hank? Do you need a burp, honey?"

I remove Hank's sunglasses.

"No," I say. "No."

Then I break those goddamn sunglasses into a half-dozen tiny pieces.

SPARE

COLUMBUS 1999

Game three, ninth frame. Boomer Nash rubs a cheesecloth bag of rosin on the webbing between his thumb and forefinger and dries his hand over the little vent in the ball return. When his hand dries, he picks up his ball, a sweet Hammer.

He steps to the third arrow and brings the edge of his left foot into the indentation of his right. He bends his knees, raises the ball to chest level, then steadies his right arm with his hook.

He accelerates his approach as he nears the foul line. The ball kisses wood and gathers speed. His hand flips up, his right foot sweeps behind. The ball arcs at the gutter, hangs on the edge, then breaks.

He waits—it's bad luck to break the pose early. The pins ricochet into the pin-wall and fall to the lane. He drops his arm and clenches his fist. Applause and a couple of shouts rise from the crowd, fifty strong and growing, gathered to watch a 300 in progress.

On the way to his seat, his teammates, except for Kevin, grin and pinch their fingers together like Frenchmen searching for the right word—a pantomime of his hook, upturned fingers presented as congratulations. He taps the tips as he passes.

Kevin doesn't offer his hand. "Nice shot," he says, stepping onto the lane.

Boomer raises his finger toward the lady in the short skirt who floats by the pub window, waiting for yelps from thirsty bowlers. She brings him a double Jack. He pays, swallows, then rests the empty glass on the wedge of speckled Formica between his and Kevin's chairs.

Kevin left the nine and ten—not his night. He sets his approach for a spare. Boomer hears him release. The ball hums as it breaks at the two remaining pins. A dreadful, hollow sound issues on impact, like a high note struck on an out-of-tune piano. Kevin whispers curses; he left the ten.

For his part, Boomer's bowling a hell of a series: 240 and 220 so far, but he can't keep his mind in the game. It keeps wandering homeward, to Vicky and Caleb, but mostly Vicky, who until this afternoon had been his villain.

Before he left for work at Biggy Sports this morning, she noticed his truck parked half up on the lawn. First, she beat him with plain language: he was fucking up his life and her life and Caleb's too with booze and bowling and regret, like his mother Ginny fucked hers on booze and cock.

Then Vicky demanded last night be the last night, and beat him with her open hand, twice across his jaw. He didn't return fire, not like he usually would've, in measured blows. He felt sheepish and guilty, like for once he deserved a beating. Her blows stung so true he hadn't the sack to deny them.

"Boomer?"

Vicky made him late, but it was still early enough that there were no customers when he arrived. Four part-time community college boys tossed a yellow Nerf ball around the shoe department. Counting the service desk drawer, Kevin asked Boomer why he was late; Kevin didn't even say hello. Boomer muttered Vicky, as if her name excused murder.

Kevin added that Boomer looked like shit and, further, smelled of booze. Boomer admitted to having been out after practice, at Lane Low. Boomer was no use hungover, Kevin said, gesturing at the boys frolicking in the shoe department. Kevin told him to go home—they were overstaffed anyhow, and it would be better for Boomer to get some sleep so he wouldn't fuck up tonight. He didn't sound as sincere as Boomer would've liked.

Boomer told Kevin he needed the hours. Kevin shrugged and told him to watch the counter while he went to the bank. The boys in the back cheered loudly, lobbing Hail Marys across the store, oblivious to the presence or absence of customers, of Kevin, or Boomer.

Boomer stood in the center aisle scratching his forehead with the hook, amused and disbelieving. A boy launched a new pass from the shoe department, toward the front door. Another sprinted backward, toward Boomer. That kid had his left arm drawn into the sleeve of his polo shirt. Running, he roared: "Boomer-catch! Boomer-catch!"

When Kevin returned, Boomer told him he'd take that offer to leave.

"Boomer?"

When she saw he'd returned, Vicky closed the checkbook and lay the stack of bills in the Dutch Masters cigar box. She dressed and left without her face on, leaving him with Caleb, who'd watched their fight last night, crying, his arm out like a little traffic cop whose beat was sending words this-way-and-that. Most of the time, Caleb kept his left arm stuffed in the left leg of his pants, out of sympathy for Boomer.

Boomer removed his harness and prosthetic and stretched out on the couch, moping. He heard the familiar swish of Pokemon footie pajamas, advancing: Caleb flung himself over, tucking his head between Boomer's stump and the couch back. He asked Boomer why he'd come home so late last night. Boomer ignored the question. Caleb asked if he was an alcoholic. He said no, a lie. Caleb said Vicky said he was. She was worried and called a policeman.

"Mom asked him about crashes and trucks, and I was scared you were in a crash, but the officer told Mom there weren't any crashes with trucks. Then she got mad. I'm glad you didn't crash, Dad."

Caleb yawned and Boomer nudged him closer with his nub. He waited until he was sure Caleb was sleeping before he wept.

"Boomer!"

Last night, shrieking, Vicky raised the accident that snatched away his NFL expectations when they'd been just within grasp. She was as bitter about it as he was. He loathed talking about college. It required framing every present action in tragedy and disappointment.

Seven years gone since they married at the little chapel between a strip joint and casino in Windsor. Six-and-a-half since he rolled his Camaro four times off a cloverleaf merging onto I-70 outside Columbus. His left forearm, good for little besides balance, aesthetics, and protecting pigskin in the bend of his arm, was sheared cleanly from his arm by the open T-tops.

Vicky was pregnant, but even through her morning sickness she accompanied him to physical therapy four hours a day, trying her best to look supportive as he learned to use the hook. It was hardly state of the art, but it was the best they could afford when the university insurance expired.

Calls stopped: the press, the agents, the scouts. Coaches stopped fawning, students ceased genuflecting, cousins and uncles in Toledo stopped trolling for tickets. Everything. It all stopped. Everything stopped but life. Coach moved Kevin to running back. Kevin acted like he'd won the lottery, going so far as to throw himself a party. He had the gall to invite Vicky and Boomer.

That's when Vicky started calling Kevin cocksucker, even to his face. Kevin wasn't pro material. Boomer's bad luck was Kevin's good fortune, but Kevin made nothing of it. Now who gives a damn who's at running back, or who's got MANAGER on his shirt—who, but Kevin?

State recruited them from Canal Winchester, where they'd been best friends. Kevin was irreplaceable, a boy who had been present at all the events in his life Boomer could recount later, glory days tales, glimmering red moments that fade each year, like the party where Boomer lost his cherry; wrestling season junior year, when Kevin took a tapeworm in a pill capsule to make weight—in a week he looked like a famine victim, sick as a dog, and couldn't wrestle at all. Kevin's doc gave him meds to kill the worm. They waited eagerly for the coming bowel movement. When Kevin delivered, they snapped a Polaroid—it was two feet long, flat and black-eyed, coiled like a sleeping cobra in Kevin's parents' toilet. Or the morning of their first two-a-day freshman year when Coach McIntosh had a flashback to Nam and kept asking if they were tired, did they feel like dying, didn't they hear the Hueys, and didn't they know Charlie was watching them right, fucking, now?

That season, after the papers noticed Boomer, Kevin's snarky asides began—little jabs: part-compliment, part-whine. As with all old friends, they had shorthand for shared notice: cryptic gestures, quizzical facial expressions, and enthusiasm—measured or unleashed—replaced words.

Swapping ideas and emotions this secret way was worth more than money, but not, it seems, more than jealousy or the pride it serves.

In the tenth frame, he sees Vicky and Caleb in the crowd. Caleb presses his left hand under his shirt, in the waist of his jeans. Boomer waves. Caleb mouths, "Hi, Daddy" and returns the wave. Vicky bids a stare. She thinks bowling's a stand-in for football, which it is, and she will not play second fiddle to yet another sport, especially one with no future, nothing for wife and baby but long evenings missing husband and daddy that end with drunken daddy's return, stumbling, polyester-shirted, smelling of fried food, cigarette smoke, and hooch.

Football was one thing. There was a future. Boomer had been pro material. But this? This shit is bowling. Even if he were excellent (he is) and even if, God forbid, he went pro (not out of the question, not entirely, no), he would still be a fucking bowler.

It's not just the bowling that pisses her off: bowlers drive her crazy. Like golf and fishing, bowling doesn't require fitness; it's an excuse to drink. It would be fine if that were all, but Boomer invests money and hope, too. This displeases her, and he knows it. She will not be a dutiful bowling widow. She says it, so he believes it. He wasn't sure if he cared until tonight.

"Boomer!?"

"What?" He snaps. "Goddammit! What?"

"Your turn."

Boomer performs his ablutions and steps onto the lane. He's careful, in a sportsman's superstitious way, to repeat everything as he has the previous nine frames. Third arrow. Feet together. Ball raised, steadied with the hook. He imagines the pocket twice its actual size. As he steps forward, the crowd gasps so loudly and distinctly they sound as if they're breathing with one mouth. He hopes Vicky's biting her thumb, like they say she used to when he ran the ball.

His thumb lingered too long on the release. The ball breaks too soon, crashing into the one instead of hitting the one and three. The pins clap like he's thrown a strike, but two pins remain: the seven and ten. The crowd groans. He walks back to the ball-return, where Kevin waits, frowning, thumbs-up.

"Bummer, bro. Goal posts."

Boomer salutes the applauding crowd with his prosthetic, then turns and warms his hand on the vent, waiting for his ball. Boomer looks past Kevin, to Vicky, squatting beside Caleb, probably explaining the split.

"Play it safe," Kevin warns. "Get the ten."

The return spits his Hammer, and Boomer takes the deck, bends his knees, and eyes the left third of the seven. *Graze the seven to slide it sideways, tap the ten.* He aims his foot left of the center arrow, presenting the ball; an offering, to some potbellied, polyester-clad god.

Boomer delivers the ball, but instead of watching the lane, he turns and watches Kevin's face. Kevin grips the back of a scorekeeper's chair so tight his knuckles have turned ice gray.

The ball breaks; a faint tap—Boomer knows that tap— the seven tipping sideward Vicky raises to her forehead as if checking a fever, which, in a way, she is. When the ten falls, the crowd bellows. Caleb strikes his right hand against his leg. Even Vicky applauds. Blood rushes Boomer's face, but Kevin's wipes white. He drops his chin and sweeps his fist across his torso. Then he forces a smile and soft-claps.

The waitress weaves through the spectators, holding a brown, cork-bottom tray, which carries three fingers of Jack, elixir of white men desirous of an excuse to misbehave. Deceptive, it assumes the squat shape of the glass it occupies. In present form, it appears harmless, a simple amber liquid: spillable, soppable, absorbable, moppable.

There is no way of telling what Jack Daniel's sour mash whiskey really intends—to speed through the bloodstream like a Viking ship bent on plunder; the booze arrives at the brain, unsuspecting, where it kicks down the blood/brain barrier to rape and pillage both synapse and superego, until it seems entirely reasonable that furniture be broken, larger men accosted, classic rock songs belted out, strange women propositioned, and rusty Ford F-150s driven sixteen miles in a haze and parked with one set of wheels on the street and the other in the front yard.

The waitress descends the steps. "On the house," she says. Vicky glares; Caleb bites his lip. He may not understand, but knows something's amiss, that it concerns him, concerns them all, and he intends to give it all the worry he can muster. Boomer whispers. "This one's yours."

The waitress throws the shot back, swallowing in one gulp. She doesn't try to suppress the twisted grimace that follows a whiskey shot. She licks her upper lip, turns, and raises her arm. The crowd erupts.

His teammates rise, rest their hands on his shoulders. He could fall backward and they would catch him; the thought delights him. A chorus of attaboys envelopes him. Beyond: there they are, Vicky and Caleb, faces flushed and happy.

Kevin waits before the trio of steps leading away from the lanes, blocking the way. "Got lucky there at the end," he says. "Too bad about the three hundred. Recall that series I rolled last season? About as good, I'd say. Almost perfect too. Once in a lifetime, man. Damn shame. Probably never come again."

Boomer pushes him aside, climbs the first step, then stops.

"Kevin," he calls over his shoulder.

"Yup?"

"You really are a cocksucker."

Vicky and Caleb wait between a chatty golf arcade game and a pair of squat pleather chairs. Vicky nibbles her thumbnail. Caleb's knees twitch, and he jabs the air with his free arm.

"Daddy knocked those pins down. The Champ!"

He tousles Caleb's hair; Caleb giggles. People stop and congratulate Boomer; he thanks them. Vicky grazes her fingertips along the curve of Boomer's prosthetic. Wicked, evergreen, her eyes, the eyes of a seductress, framed now in crow's feet, but still aglow at the iris-edges, their shine sharp enough to cut; he'd forgotten how green and deckled brown and flecked with gold they were. Her face, once pink, rounded and girlish, had gone macular, paling into fine mother's marble. Each delicate crease told a tale: toilet trainings, night feedings, pickings-up, droppings-off, parent-teacher conferences, trips to pediatricians, to Orthotists and Prosthetists, doctor-therapist conferences, waitings-up for Boomer to return safe, and on his return enduring his retching and puking, face planted in a place meant for shitting. The sight of her burns his soul.

He presses his hook into the toe of his shoe and unties it with his good hand. He repeats the process with his left. His left middle toe, pink and naked, pokes from a hole in his sock.

"Caleb, put daddy's shoes in that chair."

Caleb pinches his nose. "They stink."

Boomer puts on a stern daddy face, and Caleb places the shoes on the chair. Boomer reaches behind his neck, pinches his bowling shirt on the collar, and pulls it over his head. Naked from the waist up, he tosses the blue shirt into the chair, atop his shoes. It lands, left shoulder up, displaying his name stitched in white cursive. A silent witness, words etched on a tombstone's face.

Vicky says: "Boomer, people are watching."

He hooks her waist, pulls her in, and fastens his lips on hers. She resists, then surrenders when it's clear he won't let go. Her lips are soft, firm, but given. She clutches his back, fingers stretched across the straps of his harness. A first kiss, again.

"Let's go home," she says. Her voice is heat and smoke.

"Yes, let's."

"What about your bag and ball, Daddy?"

"Kevin can have them," Boomer says.

Caleb reaches for Boomer's hook, but Boomer bats the boy's hand away. Slowly, Caleb understands. He removes his left hand from his pants-waist and wraps his fist around the hook.

On the drive home, Boomer's throat is dry for drink, but the night air streams warm through the open passenger window, a balm on his naked torso. Still holding Caleb's hand over the center console, Boomer lowers the window farther and turns his face to the wind. It's now and he's alive and unfettered amid his wife and son, and Vicky looks straight ahead, humming as she drives.

The World and a Room Away

Washington, D.C. 1969

When her pupils adjust, Tonya Nash realizes she's staring at Abraham Lincoln's upturned boot. He peers down, lips rising at the corners. Chiseled rows relieve his face, hair, and beard. They're deepcut and extreme, as if dug with a plowshare. Blue, green, and yellow rays bleed through the skylight; they bend around the swags and bows of his body, draping him in alternating ribbons of light and shadow. The wall behind is inscribed:

IN THIS TEMPLE
AS IN THE HEARTS OF THE PEOPLE
FOR WHOM HE SAVED THE UNION
THE MEMORY OF ABRAHAM LINCOLN
IS ENSHRINED FOREVER.

Outside, at the bottom of the steps, hippies yell, "Peace now! Peace now! Peace now!"

Tonya puts her hand in the front pocket of her jean skirt. Her fingertip skates the telegram's edge. Goose pimples spread along the nape of her neck. Her sister, Ginny, stands beside, one eye closed, holding a five-dollar bill to compare the illustration on the back to the real thing. She blows a big bubble of grape gum and pops it. The walls amplify the report; it's a clean pop, like a pistol shot.

"It's better in person," she says, gathering pink threads from the corners of her mouth. "I like this one better than Jefferson's. His was too open and close to the water. This one's creepy. Is Lincoln in here?"

"He's buried out west, but he's Kentucky born."

Ginny turns to look at the fussing protestors; she's a troublemaker, homesick for trouble.

"You want to go and watch them fools? I bet they riot. I hope the police use tear gas." She squats, wrapping her fingers into the shape of a gun. Her thumb winks with each shot. "*Pow! Pow! Pow!* Mind if I go? I'll stay with you if you want." She rises to tiptoes and rubs Tonya's shoulder, but looks past and beyond. "I think the news is down there."

"Go on. I'll be down right-now-in-a-minute."

Tonya withdraws the yellow paper from her skirt and unfolds it. She holds it outward, as if calling the statue to account for the telegram's existence. Her hands shake as she scans the words.

> WESTERN UNION754A EST MAY 17 69
> CTA042ACTWAO82 AG XV GOVT PDB 9 EXTRA
> FAX WASHINGTON DC MR. ERROL MULLINS, SR.
> DON'T PHONE, CHK DAILY CHGS ABOVE 75 CTS
> DON'T DEL BTWN 10 PM AND 6 AM
> REPORT DELIVERY

When she comes to the meat she reads aloud:

> EBB HOLLER KY. THE SECRETARY OF THE ARMY
> HAS ASKED ME TO INFORM YOU THAT YOUR
> SON, SPECIALIST ERROL MULLINS JR WAS
> WOUNDED IN ACTION IN VIETNAM NEAR AP BIA
> ON MAY 14 1969 WHEN THE AREA CAME UNDER
> ATTACK BY HOSTILE FORCE. FURTHER REPORTS
> WILL BE FURNISHED. KENNETH G. WICKHAM
> MAJOR GENERAL USA 105-114 THE ADJUTANT
> GENERAL DEPT OF THE ARMY WASHINGTON DC (740).

If she can trust this twopenny onionskin, her brother's still alive, but she's furious the extent of his wounds remain untold. Half knowing's worse than knowing. Tonya folds the telegram again and slides it into her skirt. She centers herself before the idol, thick soled black shoes pressed together at the heels, heavy patent leather purse over her midriff.

If Mr. Lincoln were really sitting there she'd warn him how useless it is to be good unless you feel like dying young. She'd tell him Nixon's guaranteed long life, as much of an asshole he is. Lincoln's problem was he tried to do right by people. All they did for the trouble was shoot him in the head. Cuss this backward world; for once, people ought to get what's coming. She'd advise Lincoln that if he'd brewed corn liquor and run a whorehouse instead of saving the Union he'd have lived to be a hundred and ten. Then she'd do a shot of bourbon with him and kiss him on his leathered neck.

"Wanted tell you I'm sorry. Briar to briar."

A sloppy, white, suburban family bursts through the columns. The kids, a blond boy and girl, enter first. They run around her in figure eights, playing tag for a few seconds before making an attempt to scale Lincoln's right leg. Their parents shuffle in, breathless and loaded like pack mules with tote bags, a 35mm camera, the wife's purse, umbrellas (useless on a day like this), four collapsible lawn chairs, and a plaid picnic blanket. The children rave; the parents pause, resting. They can leave behind damage done by the children. The children seize the moment to misbehave, bringing one of the Old Man's sayings to mind: *everybody owns a thing, nobody does; call something public, you call it a mess.*

Tonya exits through the colonnade. The smell of spring changing to summer rides the crosswind. The horizon holds the slightest threat of weather, but the clouds look pent up, as if Congress passed a resolution banning them from the

Capitol. At the bottom of the steps, the protest wanes. Only a few dozen hippies remain.

Two women and a man hold white picket signs bearing words painted with broad black brushstrokes. One sign reads: PIGS KILL BABIES. Another reads: R. NIXON = A. HITLER. The man's sign reads PEACE NOW. They yell louder as their numbers drop, raising their voices at the end of each canned phrase to mask the fact that their bulk has wandered off to play Frisbee, buy hotdogs, or smoke dope. They smell of patchouli oil.

One of the chant leaders has Ginny distracted—a black-headed fellow wearing work boots, faded bell bottoms and a blue football jersey with a big 69 silkscreened on front. She leans in, tucking strands of straggly reddish hair behind her ear as he talks. By the looks of it, she agrees more with him than Tonya's ever seen Ginny agree with anybody. But that's not saying much. He sees Tonya before Ginny does. He greets her.

"You must be Mountain Girl, I heard about you from your sis, here—"

Ginny spins, grinning like she found a dollar.

"Tonya, meet Ray. He's a hippie."

"I'm not into labels," he grins.

"Ginny, we need to go. There's other stuff to see."

"What's going on?" Ray asks.

"We're going to the White House," Ginny says. "Tim Lee Carter gave us tickets. He did it to get us out of his office, I think. Tonya, you want some gum?"

Tonya glares. Ginny talks too much. Ray opens his arms, managing to seem aggressive and vulnerable at the same time. He reminds her of a Fuller Brush man: polite at first, foot-in-the-door desperate when rejected. Tonya slides the purse up her forearm, crosses her arms, and turns her back on them.

She has neither the time nor inclination to deal with Ginny's ad-lib courting. Ginny should know better.

"Tim Lee Carter your Rep? That's groovy. What's left to see? I'm a native, man. I can be your tour guide. Capitol? Library of Congress? Ford's Theater? Say the word."

"We're going to see Washington's Monument," Tonya says.

"You can come with Ginny. You ain't coming with me."

Ray waves goodbye to his gang, who seem nicer than people who make wordplays on Nixon and Hitler should. They walk beside the tall oaks and maples flanking the reflecting pool. In the distance, Washington's obelisk pierces the sky. Tonya walks stilted, nervous, half a step ahead of Ginny and Ray.

They interview one another; boring chatter, but she listens anyway. Ginny's accent is heavier than normal. On purpose. Ginny plays Southern belle, and the affectation makes Tonya furious. Hearing Ginny pimp her accent is like watching *The Beverly Hillbillies*.

"You drive up?"

"Bus."

"Seeing the sights?"

"We came to see the Pres—"

"Shut your mouth," Tonya snaps.

She grabs Ginny by the arm and pulls her away. Ginny resists just enough for both to tell she's uncooperative. He raises his right hand, palm out.

"Hey, be cool."

"Why don't you leave us alone? Just go, will you?"

"You don't mean that," he grins. "You're too uptight. I understand. It's the Pentagon, man. It's ancient. A five-pointed symbol of evil. We tried to levitate that shit back in the day. Ginsberg was here and everything. And it's very right now. You feel bellicose. I dig. It's totally normal."

Tonya leans into the soft incline at the monument's base. Flags mounted on poles circling the base rip and crackle. Her gaze follows the tapered shaft to the little black portals hewn in the peak. A red light sits atop the monument, blinking. On, off, on, like a police car's rotators. The monument makes her feel vaguely guilty, like she's caught an old-timer with his britches down, pulling his pud.

"There ain't even a question of what that's getting at," she says.

"Art's supposed to be dirty," Ginny says.

"Egyptians made them for important events," Ray explains.

"Know just about everything, don't you?"

He winks. "I know from phallic symbols."

"I bet a man would," she says.

He offers shelter. Tonya refuses, though they have no other place to stay but the YWCA. Ginny thinks shacking up with a hippie would be keen; she has not been looking forward to the Y.

She plans to pout—that much is obvious. Weary, Tonya yields. They go to Ray's flat on the second floor of a brownstone off Washington Circle. When they arrive, Ray offers to take their purses. Ginny allows him to stow hers in his bedroom. Tonya keeps hers close, nestled against her hip.

Ray's apartment is stuffy and uncomfortable. The cracked ceiling sags and someone has painted the baseboards orange. Through a storm of static on the transistor radio, Neil Diamond belts the chorus to "Sweet Caroline." Braided clouds of strawberry incense sway in soft yellow light.

A ridiculous oversized Nixon campaign poster hangs on the back of a closet door. Nixon's smile drips, false and perverse. Ray's couch lies under mounds of old newspapers, so they sit on the hardwood, backs against the wall. He makes a joke about them being too young to drink, then gives them Little Kings.

Ginny points at the poster.

"What you got him up there for?"

"Darts. My roomate and I have a way to keep score and everything. See that tooth? The one colored in? That's a bulls-eye. Nose, lips, cheeks and chin, twenty points. Hair, eyes, or collar you get ten. The rest of the body, five."

"Where's your roommate?" Tonya asks.

"Working on a farm in Virginia."

"I'd like to throw a dart in Nixon's face for real," Ginny says.

She looks worried Tonya might steal Ray's attentions, which Tonya has no intention of doing. Tonya decided on the mall she didn't care about Ginny's blabbing. An afternoon with Ray has proven stoned hippies may be annoying, but they're harmless.

"Like, you got to watch that shit. Big Brother listens, dig? I can't stand the bastard either, but you can't go around saying you'll hurt him, even if you want to. There's, like, a law and everything."

"I guess he didn't send your brother to Vietnam," Tonya says. "He ain't worried about sending ours. Makes me sick to my stomach."

"I don't have a brother. I got drafted, though."

"What you doing here?" Ginny asks.

"Better things to do than fight some fucked-up war. Serving my country right here man, out in the streets, fighting the Man."

"Our brother lives in Ohio," Ginny says. "He drives a semi in the army. We visited his wife last summer. He sends us letters sometimes, and money. They got a brick house."

A brick house means something. Most Slocum County houses seemed built with movement figured into the plan, patched from whatever materials were available—cardboard, tin, particleboard, canvas, you-name-it. Everybody's waiting upon something terrible, certain to come but still unknown, after which they'll flee, getting out of the mountains while there's still getting to be got. Brick house means you stay where you are.

"Only the one boy in your family?"

"Christ, no," Tonya snickers. "We could field a ball team. Not that we would."

"Can you imagine the Old Man coaching?" Ginny says to Ray: "The Old Man is our father."

"Can't coach with a horsewhip and bad intentions," Tonya says. "Your father, anyway. I disowned him."

Ray wears the visible discomfort of somebody from a good family hearing people from a bad family being honest about their kin.

"Heavy, man. So, you're going to the White House tomorrow. What then? You going back to, where is it?"

Tonya: "Slocum County."

"You going back there?"

"We had one-way tickets," says Ginny, extending her thumb. "I'll probably hitch."

"Little young to go all over hitching?"

"Ain't you a little old to give us beers?"

"Touché," he says. "You know you probably won't see him tomorrow, right? The President isn't usually there. Even when he is, he doesn't speak to tours. Especially Nixon. He's paranoid as shit."

"I didn't say I wanted to speak to him." Tonya mutters.

"Pardon me, ladies," Ray begs.

He pads down the hallway. The bathroom door closes; a fan whirs.

"You're so hung up on Junior," Ginny says.

Tonya whispers back, speaking behind her hand like she's telling a secret. Her voice trembles, her chin quivers, and then her eyes glaze, rimmed radish pink.

"I don't want to air laundry in front of some hippie."

"He can't hear over that fan. He won't remember anyway—half the time hippies are stoned."

"Junior's the only one don't know to look at me funny." She removes the telegram from her skirt, waving it under Ginny's nose.

"There was one person I didn't have to hide from. Now," she waves the telegram at the poster, "that fat-nosed fucker's messed it up. Gooks didn't do shit to Junior. I blame Nixon. You know Mama took to calling me a whore?"

Ginny laughs, pointing at her own chest. "But that's crazy. I'm the whore."

She waits for the mood to lighten, but Tonya doesn't let it; she's happy just to have beaten tears. Ray returns, folded blankets in hand, a pillow under his arm. Tonya stows the telegram.

"Hey, ladies. Sorry I went MIA. Call of the wild, you dig?" His head lolls back. Softly, he bays: "*Owwww!* Anyway. It's getting late. I brought some covers." He produces a baggie of marijuana. "Want a nightcap?"

Tonya says no and takes the blankets. Ginny says yes and asks for rolling papers. Ray hands her a box of Zig-Zags, from which she pulls a sheet. Squeezing the edges of the paper between her fingers, she makes a little trough and sprinkles the herb inside.

"You know, what? Marijuana's Kentucky's biggest crop."

Steel on flint; inhalation, exhalation. Tonya puts the newspapers from the couch onto the floor and spreads her bed. The cushions smell of mildew and cat piss. She crawls into the folds of the couch, hiding her purse beneath her, and pulls the blankets over her shoulders. A thick mist of weed smoke permeates the air.

"You have a cat?"

"Got rid of him," Ray says. "He kept spraying everywhere." Ray and Ginny chuckle and scoot around, conspiring. The room goes dark. A door opens in the hallway. For a time, there is silence, then Tonya hears a mischievous bevy of happy sounds emanate from Ray's bedroom—the rustling bodies negotiating small space: fidgeting, settling, twisting bed sheets.

The murmurs yield to an irregular rhythm on the box springs, joined by Ginny's moans and Ray's staccato grunts. Tonya shudders. Their lowing is animal, terrible. She forces herself to sleep, but the rest is fitful, and she dreams of Egypt.

Ray wakes them early and offers fare to the White House, but Tonya refuses, citing pride and the money in her purse. Ginny is already dressed and showered, wearing yesterday's clothes and shame, but not much else. He kisses Ginny on the cheek and encourages them to leave, but apologizes for doing it. Tonya rises, grabs her purse, and goes to the bathroom, which reeks of Hai Karate. She splashes water on her face and arranges her hair in a barrette. The mirror returns a sallow mugshot.

They wait on his stoop. Tonya taps her foot and drums her fingers on the wrought iron banister. It's warm this morning, and little pink buds hang bunched on the drooping tree branches. No wind stirs them; the world holds its breath.

"You enjoy yourself?"

"The weed was good. The boy?—so-so."

"Most are," Tonya takes a beat. "You don't have to come with me."

"I came this far, didn't I?"

It's the answer she wants, but she's ashamed for wanting it. Tonya's afraid of being alone with her mind. Having someone nearby, someone she knows and who knows her, feels like proof of sanity.

A white cab with a checkerboard on the door arrives, recklessly, piloted by a brown man whose forehead lies in twisted cotton. They hire him, climb inside. Ginny asks him where he's from. He says, East Pakistan, then asks *where to?* They tell him the White House.

As they pull into traffic, dread descends from Tonya's throat into her stomach. She tries to control it, and trains her concentration on the coarse stitching on the back of the driver's seat, but it's no use. Her breath whistles in her throat, quick and labored, and her state seems to concern Ginny, because Ginny tries to make her laugh by asking the driver rude questions about his hat and whether East Pakistan is that place they eat dogs, or that other place, where they worship cows.

She tips the driver well. She identifies with him. He is a stranger in this land, too. Plus, he put up with Ginny's mouth. It doesn't matter whether he ate dogs back home or if he looks like a Q-tip in that turban. Anybody who can suffer Ginny Nash's tirades deserves respect and hazard pay.

Also, there's the odd strands of fate weaving fates, regardless of skin, headgear, or food. Someday a reporter or some professor might ask him about her. She wants him to say nice things. Last thing she wants is to go down in history as a cheapskate.

The cab rolls away, leaving them before a tall iron fence that ends in a grey stone hut. Middle-aged men stand about, their faces mean and lazy. A dozen pale mustaches on pink upper lips; hidden under blazers, full-blown beer guts, or pudgy hints of beer guts underway, hang over belts. Shoulder holsters bulge just below left armpits. Comic forms, serious jobs. They lean, posed confidently; they wave VIPs in, and stop the less familiar to demand credentials.

Uniformed officers stand nearby: among them, a colored man. Tonya wonders who he knew to get a job where all you do is stand around looking tough and shiny in a blue suit and captain's hat, wearing a gleaming, long barreled .38 on your hip. Must be nice to know you have a gun ain't ever going to be used. Must be like wearing jewelry.

"What time you got?"

Ginny looks at her watch. "Nine."

She holds iron fence posts in her fists and peers through the bars at the White House. Tonya follows her stare: the gardeners have planted a ring of red flowers around the rippling fountain; the first-floor window awnings alternate, cusped, then arched. A rooftop flag pitches gently. The air holds a whiff of salt.

"There it is. The Executive Mansion. The People's House. Home of Richard Milhous Nixon, President of these United States of America. Think we'll see him?"

"I hope," Tonya says. "Then again, I hope not."

"You'll be famous, Tonya. In a bad way. Like John Wilkes Booth or Lee Harvey Oswald. I ain't saying you should, I ain't saying you shouldn't. You ought to know, that's all."

"People loved Kennedy. They loved Lincoln. Booth and Oswald were political. This here's personal."

"Somebody loves Nixon. He won."

"Money and guns and bullheadedness elected him."

"Keep telling yourself. For every red-blooded, Christian, American heart, there's a puckered, Christian, American asshole. Can't have one without the other. And the asshole's louder." Ginny checks her watch again. "Almost a quarter after. Let's go, if you're going."

They step into line behind a gaggle of tourists congregated at the guard shack. Tonya's purse dangles, heavy, from her arm. She moves to adjust it; the movement catches the colored officer's attention. He locks his wide brown eyes on her, raises a radio from his belt, and speaks into it. His glare never leaves her.

The men turn their gazes to her, one-by-one, all on her, and the heavy black purse. She backs away, but when she moves, they move also. She hears steps now, approaching from behind, coming now, growing louder, the ominous click-clack of varnished beat cop shoes. The colored officer raises his chin, a signal to someone behind her. He unlatches the catch on his holster and wraps his fingers around the pistol grip. Ginny waves both her hands, like she's dropped something hot.

"Oh, shit!"

Unzipping her purse, Tonya lurches at Pennsylvania Avenue. A nickel-plated Model 29 Smith & Wesson .44 lies in the handbag, between a pack of Kleenex and two perforated, pale green Greyhound ticket stubs. The gun weighs three pounds. Lugging it around has been like toting a poodle. She reaches for it.

But they're on her. They tear the purse from her arm. The colored officer wraps Ginny in a bear hug. Tackled from behind, Tonya drops the gun. It rattles across the concrete. Someone, a woman, screams.

Tonya's sight fades. It's dark now; her lungs strain and her ribs strain to hold form, but they give way. The pain is almost nice, it's surely welcome—to feel something, even pain, is better than to feel nothing.

She comes to in the back of a sedan, cuffed, and they're speeding past Lincoln's temple. Mind reeling, images crash over her: Lincoln enthroned, slaves hoisting an obelisk, poor, white trash building houses from castoff tin and particleboard; the Old Man arched over her, penetrating her sex, his body sweaty, blackened in coal dust, unbathed from the mines;

brothers sobbing, eyes in handkerchiefs or bandanas while the Old Man screeches for them to watch; Mama in the kitchen, peeling taters, whistling "I'll Fly Away" through the whole thing, the world and a room away.

Imageless emotion follows, pinned to color—freedom dangerous; submissive rosy pink; ashen dread. Soft green contentment, mixed with a queer sense of liberty born in irony. Being taken prisoner in body frees her soul. She's going somewhere without mines, without the Old Man, away from the unsure, darting eyes of brothers who know things they wish they didn't.

Her face feels bruised and swollen. Between complaints aimed at the front seat about her handcuffs being too tight, Ginny informs Tonya her bottom lip looks like a full hot water bottle. The broad-shouldered men in front ignore Ginny's complaints. The girls are cargo, beneath response.

"Ginny, did you tell anybody why we came?"

Silence.

"Ginny."

Ginny tears up.

"It was just pillow talk, Tonya."

All this is happening to someone else, not her, some character in a movie, a book, somebody in a newspaper, the friend of a cousin. Flying, flying now—here's the black sedan, below—she soars above the Lady of Freedom, past the Washington Monument, across the reflecting pool, back to the warm womb of Lincoln's Memorial, safe in the granite. She climbs the statue, stands on her tiptoes to caress Lincoln's sorrow-wizened face, and confesses her sins and the wretched sins of others, briar to briar.

They pull her from the car, hands firm around the tallow of her upper arm. Their touch is a distant itch. Ginny struggles and wails, but Tonya puts one foot in front of the other, jaw firm, chin up, proud. She knows now what she'd whisper in Abraham Lincoln's ear: she'd tell him sometimes the free are captives, and sometimes the captives are free.

ALL THINGS OLD MUST PASS AWAY

EDDYVILLE 1979

This week Liney's been up at seven every morning, outside the mine, stretching to the tick-tack of an old fellow walking the line, tapping cross ties with a walking stick. If he catches Liney, he's sure to wave; more often than not, the old fellow misses him.

Liney spends the evenings drawing pictograms in the dirt, or experimenting on the backs of paper grocery sacks with the negative space possibilities of coal dust, which, to his delight, acts just like charcoal. It took four long nights to overcome his animal fear of the dark.

The mine teems with life. If he's sought refuge within, why wouldn't bats, rattlesnakes, or bobcats? He keeps his lantern ready. When he hears movement in the chamber, he spotlights the area. Nothing's ever there.

On the fourth night he sleeps soundly, bowed like a fetus, one hand beneath his chest, the other cradling his head, his forearm a pillow. Blood thumps in the veins of his arm; coursing, he can hear it. If he had a mind he could take his own pulse.

The next night Wayne sneaks a pile of moth-ridden blankets up from the house. Now he's comfortable, he's decided. A thing among things, at home among his fellow nocturnal creatures. On night six, the weary remnants of a Carolina hurricane blow through the holler. It's hard to tell the difference between the sound of the rustling pines twisting outside the mine's mouth and the noisy adjustments of invisible critters. He closes his eyes, waiting, listening for the wind to climax and burst into wet relief.

Then it hits him, fast and hard as the Old Man's hand: a silent watcher shares the cave, a human, hiding ten feet back in the shaft, in the body of a broken-down elevator surrounded by an iron cage. Some region of his mind has accounted for the intruder's presence without him consciously recognizing it. Like mamma said: If you feel like you're being watched, you are.

He slides his hand over to the utility lamp, a weapon, to brain whomever is back there. He crouches, then takes a stilted duck walk toward the elevator. A thunderclap roils overhead, followed by a long flash that lights the mine blue. He sees a face, young and freckled, framed by tresses of meticulously feathered red hair, and beady eyes tilting downward at the corners.

"About got this lamp upside your head."

"I took the battery out while you was pissing."

Liney flicks the switch on and off, off and on, then again. Nothing. He turns back to the mine's entrance, feeling careless to have missed the change in weight. He doesn't let his guard down often; it's embarrassing when he does.

Wayne opens the cage door; the metal racket echoes through the mine, metal on metal. A dozen bats fly in, fleeing the rain. Liney sits, back against the wall. Wayne stands over him, offering the 12-volt cell.

"You'll steal anything," Liney says.

"Just trying to scare you."

Liney draws his feet under his torso. He replaces the battery. He toggles the switch and places the lamp on its end to spread the light.

"Bring any weed?"

Wayne holds a green Army surplus shoulder bag out to Liney.

"And a radio. No telling how good a signal you'll get. I got a station out of Morehead the other night, but that was down home."

Liney pulls a silver pipe, a baggie full of nuggets, and a Zippo lighter from the bag. He unscrews the cap from the pipe's end and inserts a pinch of marijuana; the weed wets his fingers, resinous and sticky.

"Good stuff," he says.

"Allen's doing hydroponics. You grow in water instead of dirt."

Liney rolls his thumb on the lighter's flint wheel, hears it strike, then tilts both the pipe and lighter sideways so that the bowl meets the flame. The hot butane burns his lungs, but then he feels the scratch of marijuana chasing the gas. He holds the smoke in his chest for as long as he can, then exhales, coughing, and passes the pipe to Wayne.

"You do this shit in the dirt? You should be an artist. Hand me that lighter."

"Don't jack me off."

"I ain't. Old Man aims to kill you, you know."

"How's his eye?"

"Still can't see."

"I hoped to put it out. And he won't kill me if I get him first."

"You'll get the chair."

"I'll tell what he did to Tonya and Mama."

Wayne passes the pipe back to Liney, who hits it again. His limbs grow long and his head inflates like a balloon. The mine extends and heightens; it's big as a gymnasium. Wayne reaches into his back pocket and pulls out a tinfoil rectangle. He holds it by the corner and waves it in the air.

"They won't believe you. Anyway, you ain't got to kill nobody. Allen Buck's got an idea. Acid, brother. Lots of it."

"What good's trippin' gonna do?"

"Allen knows somebody can get it, cheap. Mather Buck's working with a bunch of hippies in Chicago. They live in a big warehouse and fuck each other all the time. Mather told him the last time the Grateful Dead went through, the hippies made $75,000 off blotter alone. Mather'll give a book or two on credit, for cost. Break the books up and sell them. Course, that's all according to Allen."

Wayne rolls his eyes and pinches open the corner of the tin-foil square.

"This here's Mather's blotter."

"Break me off some."

They chew the doses. Liney turns the radio on and adjusts the tuning until they get a static-laden opera station on the AM band. Liney lays the radio against a lump of coal without changing the station.

"Fuck the Dead," he says.

"You can make five grand just for going, Liney. Old Man don't have to know. Get on up to Toledo and stay with Junior a spell. They say Jeep's hiring. You don't even need a diploma."

"Why don't Allen go hisself?"

"You know how he is. Gets nervous is all. He wants a big dumb hillbilly behind him when he does the deal. Makes him feel like a thug. Besides, he likes you. When he heard you whipped the Old Man, he sent these nuggets over, on the house."

The mural fades into sprayed-on, three-dimensional names, the tags of hoods and gangs, markers and claims, written so somebody knows the people who wrote them exist.

A big black fire door, tagged with a giant yellow question mark, interrupts the mural. A lean blonde slides the fire door open. She steps out, rests her palms on her hips, tilts her head to one side.

"I like your painting," Liney says.

"Right on. Merry Pranksters did the trippy stuff."

Liney's never heard of the Merry Pranksters.

"Just here for the art?"

"My cousin lives here," Allen wheezes. "You know Mather Buck."

"We came to Illinois to buy some LSD," Liney says.

The girl's face ages in quick time.

"I don't know what you're talking about," she says, nearly shouting, eyes darting to the street corners and parked cars. "But you better come in."

She leads them through a fog of smoke and a maze of rooms made from hanging sheets and upright particleboard, up a set of metal stairs to what had once been a foreman's office, with a view of the factory floor.

Inside, Mather reclines on a red beanbag, wearing a wife beater and cutoff jeans. The tip of a hookah hose dangles in the corner of his mouth. A girl wearing a tube top rubs his bare feet with cinnamon oil.

"*Hello*, Kentucky," he sings.

The cousins shake hands.

"What brings you boys up?"

The condescension stings Liney; seeing Mather's got Allen effervescent.

"Doses—"

"Wait a minute, Allen," Liney snaps. "They didn't know we was coming?"

Allen scoots an arm's length from Liney. Mather raises his eyebrows and closes his lips around the hose tip. The hookah bubbles; he looks decadent and elegant, like an Oriental potentate. Liney fumes in silence. Allen looks nervous.

Mather pats the girl on her head and suggests she excuse herself. As she leaves, she touches Liney's shoulder with her fingertips, letting the inertia pull her arm and hand and fingers across his back.

He tries to ignore her—can't tell who's hooked up, and doesn't want to start any trouble. Mather winks. Liney allows himself to believe Allen's free love tales might be true. The girl gone, Mather goes from bohemian to bond trader.

"Terms?"

"Credit," Allen says, his voice breaking. "I can turn two books in a month."

Mather motions at Liney with his thumb.

"Who's this guy?"

"Lienenkugel Nash. He's beef. I'm going to cut him in for the favor."

"Your momma name you after beer?"

"The Old Man."

"I'll think about it, since you're kin. You gonna stay all night?"

Allen and Liney exchange glances, each trying to discern an answer from the other's face before giving his own. Liney thinks of the girl rubbing his shoulders. Allen tells Mather that they'll stay.

They settle for dinner in a big room on the first floor. Everyone sits cross-legged around a squat circular table, sharing flatbread, couscous, and jug wine. Liney's beside the blonde who welcomed them. She's in his personal space with her knees and elbows, but he doesn't mind.

"You like Chicago?"

"Came straight to. Can't say I seen it."

"How about our little experiment? We're working off karma."

Liney tells her that's fine, and while he's familiar with too many people trying to live in too small a space, the sharing thing is new. She tells him life is about giving and sharing.

Across the table, Allen whispers to Mather; beside them, two fat girls explain something important to a bushy-bearded man named Wind. A girl with pigtails and a pug nose breastfeeds a fat baby. A sunbeam weaves through the west-side skylight and hits the center of the table in a trapezoidal bar, and suddenly the place unfolds.

If he had acrylics and brushes and enough time, he'd make a masterpiece of them. He'd lay them out like Leonardo's Last Supper, and portray them contented instead of fretting; with gentle strokes and good light depicting goodheartedness, the strangeness, and joy. The whole hippified setup is so tragic.

Liney has to laugh or cry, so he bursts with a full-on belly laugh and keeps laughing until the others join. He's *selling* the laugh, converting them, as if it were the only reasonable response to the absurdity of pretentious human bullshit, in Kentucky or South Side Chicago or wherever he wakes up that morning. The blonde laughs until she cries; she slaps the table and rests her other hand on his thigh.

After dinner, Mather's old lady and the blonde take him to another office in the back of the warehouse. Surrounded by piles of never-mailed invoices, rusty Burroughs adding machines, and Corona Selectrics, they burn patchouli incense and smoke up, discussing how ironic it is to party in the ruins of capitalism.

The conversation funnels downward to odd feelings and premonitions. The girls tell Liney about Nostradamus. Half an hour and two joints later, the end-of-the-world talk has him spooked. Allen rounds the corner with a grocery sack, Mather in tow, Liney's relieved.

"Good to go," he says, raising the sack. "Gonna stash this in the trunk."

Mather gives Liney a thumbs-up and pinches his thumb and forefinger as if holding an invisible joint, then flicks his head at Mather.

"We'll be outside burning a fatty."

When Allen and Mather go, Liney begs the girls to lay off eschatology.

"I don't want to talk about the Antichrist no more," he says.

The blonde rubs his arm.

"The apocalypse is beautiful, baby. It's the wheel, dying and being born again. It's an unveiling, like a bride with a lifted veil. Dig it. All things old must pass away."

The girls move in.

"Ain't you Mather's woman?"

"Property is a bourgeois construct. We don't own one another. I'm real. Matt's real. Real people have needs."

She moves against him, pressing her nipples, visibly rigid through the thin fabric of the tube top, against his arm. The blonde lowers his zipper and coos when she realizes he's commando. She weaves his dick through the flap and strokes him. Short and extremely fat, it hardens in her hand.

Mather's woman licks his neck and earlobe, offering wicked suggestions, reciting memorized quatrains and verses from Revelation. She unbuckles his belt and slides her hand into the rear of his pants, his crack, gently fingers his anus, massages his ball sack from behind.

The blonde twists his penis like a screwdriver, gripping and groping, until he blows his load over the back of her hand. His only thought as he's catching his breath is an artist's thought—that his semen shines like mother-of-pearl. Without wiping her hand, the blonde takes his wrist, and leads him down the hall.

Allen's shrieks wake Liney. Naked, he moves the blonde's arm, climbs across Mather's old lady, and peers across the sash. Allen stands below, staring at the Bonneville's remains, a handful of hair in each fist. Some thief cracked the Bonneville's steering column open and left a flathead Craftsman jammed in the ignition. Liney hops into his jeans and goes outside, shirtless and barefoot.

Hubcaps: gone; passenger-side front window: shattered; radio: yanked clean out the dash. The headlights are lit, but the battery's low, and they're dim. Weeping, Allen yanks the screwdriver from the steering column.

That's when Liney sees the glove compartment door dangling open, like a mouth in surprise. Inside, there's the giant yellow TRUNK button, a trunk that holds—or held—Mather's acid; expensive, precious, unpaid-for.

They sell the car to a scrapyard for the cost of the tow. Before dark they're on the dog, crawling southbound slowly. In the window seat, Liney watches the land swell; the rising land gives the illusion they're descending. Allen's cooking up schemes to raise the three grand they owe Mather.

Liney ignores him—he has a plan of his own. He'll kick Wayne's ass for this little adventure, then have it out once and for all with the Old Man. Mather might be a big-shot hippie acid dealer, but if Mather wants a piece of him he'll have to get in line behind Errol, Sr. Those hippie girls were right. You got to put the past behind you, or you can't move on.

Allen suggests they should rob John Johnson, the retired locomotive engineer who'd woken Liney through the week, obsessively counting off the cross ties with a walking stick. Rumor had it Johnson carried a roll in his pocket and wore more gold on his fingers than a polite fellow ought to.

They'd get good and stoned, meet him on the tracks, knock him cold, relieve him of his wallet and jewelry, then hitch to the bus station, pawn the rings in Chicago, settle with Mather, and do the sale again. Everything would be fine, just a week off schedule. Liney starts to think robbing the old man might work.

That night, Liney rests with Wayne and Allen in the mine, seated cross-legged beside the lamp and his sleeping bag. Wayne skulks over a clay bong painted like a human skull, pulling tubes. He giggles into the bong's top.

"Spics took your shit? Saw your country asses coming a mile off. Spics even trip? Don't they just smoke Mary Hwana? Cheech is spic, ain't he?"

"I didn't say it was no Mexican." Liney says. "That's you."

"They like big cars," Allen muses.

Liney changes the subject to the Old Man. "What's the temperature down there?"

"Eyesight's back."

Allen coughs and passes Liney the bong.

"That old bastard's like the wind," Allen says, twirling his finger above his head. "Tell where he's been by what he's moved."

Wayne opens the flap on the shoulder bag and withdraws two bottles and a foil square full of acid tabs from inside. He lays the remaining acid between them and hands the bottles to the boys.

"Ale-eight-one. I'm going to leave this acid. Don't need more of that shit."

Allen pops the cap from his soda.

Liney places the bong on the ground, leans over, and slaps Allen's face. The slap resounds through the mine; Allen's head snaps back—a small trickle of blood runs from his nostril. Liney hit him that hard—hand to cheek, nosebleed. The Ale-8-1 topples.

"The hell was that for?" Allen whines.

"I warned you on talking about what you don't know."

"Jesus, Liney," says Wayne. "Don't think he meant nothing." The three keep silent for a long time. Allen gestures at the bong, asking if he can hit it again.

Before they rob Mr. Johnson, Allen and Liney each eat two hits of acid. Then, for no good reason at all, Liney takes the rest of the blotter, eight hits strong, and sticks them to the roof of his mouth.

"Oh, Liney," Allen says, covering his mouth with his hand. "Why'd you do that? Shit, man. We need to take you to a hospital. They can give you a tranq. 'Ludes or something. Oh, Lord."

"We're going to do this right."

The acid leaps up, just that fast, and in minutes the mine entrance, not five feet out, seems so far away Liney's unsure he could hit it with a gun. He's worried, for the longest moment ever, that his eyeballs are melting, and running down his cheeks like tears made of molasses. Feels like somebody just blew him headfirst out of a shotgun. Blood collects in his limbs; he feels nauseated. He creeps to the mine opening—it takes so long, forever, so long, a *journey*, those five feet—and peeks out. Allen walks in a tight circle, round and round, behind him.

"I'm going to have a bad trip," he moans. "I can feel it. You want to call it off, Liney? You want to call it off? We can wait. I don't have a problem."

Liney hears a voice roaring. He knows the voice. It's not Mr. Johnson's.

I am Alpha and Omega, the beginning and the ending, which is, and which was, and which is to come.

The figure approaches, fresh from the underworld. Mountains behind no longer resemble an amalgam of mineral and vegetable, they've become pyramids—this one a step pyramid, like in Mexico, that one a smooth-sided Egyptian job. The figure, a corpse mummified, lumbers forth; the wicked thing is coming at him. He feels hot breath on his neck, Mather's woman's voice in his ear, in his head, goading him, giving him the words:

The Devil is come down unto you, having great wrath, because he knoweth that he hath but a short time. His deadly wound was healed: and all the world wondered after the Beast!

Allen sits, back on the wall, knees to his chest, rocking.

"I can do this. I can do this."

"Let's go," says Liney, his voice a droning monotone.

He steps into the light. As if sensing his emergence from the dark, the approaching figure calls:

Who is like unto the beast? Who is able to make war with him? Here is wisdom: Let him that hath understanding count the number of the Beast: for it is the number of a man; and his number is six hundred, threescore, and six.

Allen darts down the path and through the old coal yard. Rusted miners, broken and left for scrap, rear against the sky like massive insects, praying mantises, bent-armed and nefarious, scanning for prey. Allen hurdles the broken-down chain-link and webbed concertina wire, then stops and waits for Liney. The acid has taken Allen to a different place; he's a muse, a beautiful Renaissance boy, posing. Liney shouts. "When this is over, I will paint you!"

The figure is nearly on them. Liney sees his fears and hopes are true. The Old Man has come ugly and angry, without his man-costume or any pretense of humanity; wax-paper skin tight across rotten wooden bones, his staff not a walking stick, but black magic totem of discipline and torture. Coal tar drips from the corners of his mouth, and when he speaks, he sounds as if speaking underwater.

"Don't want no trouble, boys," he says.

"Lies," Liney mutters, hyperventilating.

He was born for this moment, for testing himself against the Father. Liney looks to heaven, as if receiving an epiphany, raises his foot knee-high, and brings it down on the Old Man's knee. The sky is lit orange, aflame; its color undulating across the spectrum with each heartbeat. The Old Man howls, and drops his staff across the rails.

"Knock him out," Allen grunts. "Do it, quick."

The crying Old Man rolls into a ball, holding his knee in a cradle of interlocked fingers. Liney raises the staff. It feels heavy in his hands, electric and powerful. He's surging. The Old Man hisses:

And their dead bodies shall lie in the street of the great city, which spiritually is called Sodom and Egypt, where also our Lord was crucified.

Allen kicks the Old Man—over, and over, and over. Liney brings the stick down across the Old Man's nose. The sound of the bone breaking feels like burnt toast.

"Daughter-fucker," spits Liney. "This is for Tonya!" Again, the stick across the face. "For Mama!" Again, the stick across the face. "Junior!" Again, the stick across the face. "Ginny!" Again, the stick across the face. "Penny!" Again. "For Wayne, for Cory!" Kicks, to what had minutes earlier been a human face. "Yeah," he says. "And for me, you sumbitch—for me."

The Old Man's obliterated mug looks like a dish of raw chitterlings. Disgusted, Liney tosses the wand beside the tracks. He's red to the wrists and knees; the blood splatter on his lips stings metallic.

Allen stuffs the Old Man's wallet in his back pocket. He kneels and starts on the rings.

"His fingers is too fat, Liney. I can't get his rings off."

Liney pushes Allen off and raises the Old Man's hand. He sniffs the fingers, then bites each one off, moving from pinkie to index. Where there are rings, he pulls them from his mouth and collects them in his free hand; but he swallows each finger, licking the blood from his own as he goes. Allen blinks, then removes the wallet from his pocket and tosses it on the ground at Liney's feet. He turns and runs, arms flailing, screaming that Liney ate John Johnson's fingers.

Allen's shrieking will bring the people. Liney kneels, waiting for them to come. They will take measurements and pictures and statements. They will take him away. He scoops a handful of blood from once-face, raises the cupped hand to his eye, and considers the deep claret of blood, marveling that he has never seen such a beautiful pigment in any paint.

As the world expands and contracts around him, complementing his breathing with its own, he hopes the warden lets him paint a masterpiece before they strap him in the chair; a painting he sees now, levitating in the air before him as if he needed only grab it from the ideal, and pull it into existence. In absolutely perfect perspective, the oil-on-velvet twilight highway empties into a ring of radiant white light. In the foreground, a gorgeous blonde with windblown hair stares straight ahead, toward life.

EBB HOLLER OXYCONTIN BLUES

EBB HOLLER 1999

Give Roger yer money'n take 'em pills down th' house'n get 'em up yer nose'n it'll be all right. Get down t'britches'n set up'n th' kitchen'n sniff 'em Oxys crushed up'n under a spoon till 'ey aint but powder. Take a razor'n cut three or five good lines 'pendin' how yer nose's pullin'. Suck 'em up but go easy 'cause take t'much'n gon' nod out'n miss th' buzz. Y'all wan' know th' fuss's 'bout? Ask somebody does 'em. Bes' feelin' ever, longes' hardes' come, 'at piss'n shit ye held till yer teeth hurt. Ten times it. Better'n anythin'. Oxys brings th' beauty 'cause this ol' world's s'damn ugly, get wide'n think on th' good, like 'at rope 'ey lowered th' Old Man's coffin on. Knots'n rope'n untie 'em'n retie 'em, practicin' loops like th' Old Man taught. Leave it a-lyin' on th' couch t'spook yer brother 'cause he come over too much'n ain't got nothin' good t'say. Felt good t'put 'at ol' devil in, din't it? Study 'bout folk doin' fucked up shit'n what happens t'make 'em go off'n but some mu'fuckers jus' born evil. Got luck bad 'nough t'get'n 'at game, it's sumpin' fer ye t'deal with. Get t'ye kitchen. Do 'nother few line 'en yer heart's a-breakin' 'cause it's all gon'. Pace th' livin' room back'n forth'n wish fer weed or sleepin' pills or sumpin', anythin'. Cold'n hands'n feet'n sick t'yore stomach, like ye took a touch a flu. T'fix it give Roger th' money. But ye done spent 'at money. He'll take sumpin' else? 'Em old guns ye put up. He ain't but tells ye can pawn 'em down th' Slocum County seat. Lord a'mighty: how'd life go'n get like this? Look o'er t'th'couch'n ye wonder jus' how much weight 'at ole rope'll hold.

SNOWBALL JACKSON

EBB HOLLER 1976

Opal wakes to Errol Sr. loading a 30.06 in the hall outside their bedroom. She rolls from the mattress and squeezes herself between a chest of drawers and the wall. Moonlight washes the bed, her gun, the furniture, his rifle, the floor planks, and faded photos taped to the wall in monochrome, leaving blurred margins where things may end and could begin. She removes a small gold pistol from her cleavage. She flicks the safety off.

"Raise your head," he shouts. "I'll blow the goddamn thing off your shoulders. Let me see it. Just the top. Top's all I need. Now what? This fucking thing."

He never did take to that stock. The gunsmith sanded it too thin. He can't put it to his shoulder long before it gets to hurting. So he says. Can't believe a word. She peeks around the bureau's edge and answers, trying to sound resolved.

"Fool, I got me one, too. Been to Bell County, ain't you? Them whores bend over for you?"

A shot rips the air. Kingdom Come coming. Endless echoes echoes echoes trail the blast. A bullet tears clean through the tin roof. She imagines a flurry of insulation and plaster falling on him. A clatter sounds as he drops the rifle to the floor.

"Fuck me in the ass!"

She hums—a hymn—thinking about the springtime smell of warm soup beans, boiling greens, rain. He leans on the doorframe, weight on his wrist. His head lolls. He's trying to see the elk killer in the dark.

"Lost your gun?"

"Do you with my hands if I have to."

"Souse. You can't feel your hands."

"Sure enough I can."

In a small voice: "This is the last time."

He removes his Stetson and crouches. He wipes his brow, bends, and reaches for the rifle. She scrambles the distance between them, stopping between him and the rifle. She lowers the pistol to his chin. She means it, too—ready as a human can be to kill another. Nervous, unsure, yes, but willing. She feels naked. He's a beast, feral and empty, and she loathes him.

When they ask why she stays, she answers with her own question. Where in tarnation would I go? They stopped asking. They stopped a long time ago. He's taking measure of the span between himself and the rifle, weighing a lunge, a reach around, or whether to knock her over. He brings his gaze in, staring cross-eyed down the pistol's stubby barrel.

She wavers, slackens her elbow, and lowers the pistol ever so slightly. Mistake. He hammers her forearm with a fist. She cries out and releases her grip. He yanks the pistol from her hand, pulls himself to standing, and punches her dead in the face. She recovers, then says, "When you're romping in Bell County, they ever ask? About my baby?"

"You crazy cunt. That's Dwayne Skelton's bastard."

"They ask where the girls went?"

"Where they belong."

"Big talking man. Tell them they tried to shoot Nixon? You know why they went to Washington? I know."

He pistol-whips her. She fights him, swinging wild, scratching at his eyes and nipples and kneeing at his crotch, but he's chased pills with booze. God knows which or what or how many; but it figures, then, why he's so dumb and angry and determined, despite being so stoned he can't hardly stand. He takes every blow and turns it on her double.

"Trifling's what you're! Can't hold a job. Won't pay a bill. Romp in Bell County every time you get a dollar. Lie when you can tell the truth. Gulp them pills and whip us—ain't you a big man—beat your old lady and your children. And—" Pressure builds behind her eyes, and her voice trembles. "—you know what else."

"Tonya's a whore. Said it yourself. She got done like a whore does."

On that, guilt scores her. She keeps Tonya in a box apart from sleeping and eating and breathing. She can't let fact worm between the seams that divide her heart and soul, divided for survival's sake. Facts so godawful filthy and wrapped in death's stink. If given their names, muttered even to herself alone, they're so revolting they threaten to overturn her willed-numb conscience, and put the body she kept at constant labor for distraction's sake.

Weary bones yield; industry halting—her spirit assuming what inertia her body loses, leaving her present, really present, for the first time. She'll howl in earned agony. She'd free fall inward, tumble down the well of her soul. A long pit, black, bored hollow and bottomless by long years enabling madness. Resting at last, but doomed to an unquiet mind and ruptured heart, a fate she chose when she failed to choose.

What kind of mother takes denial over her daughter?—or waits a decade to ask after a missing newborn, not long for the world, and foul and deformed, but her baby still? No kind, that's what kind. She nurses an envy and pity for Tonya that promises to crush her peace of mind, which is shaky at the best of times. If envy won't suffice, recollections of the unmourned infant boy will conjure a poison sorrow to do it instead. It's coming quick, like a downpour on thunder. The feeling chokes her like a yoke.

"I had to be mad at somebody. Lord, I wish I'd never said it."

"She's a liar. Nixon said so."

"You lie through your teeth. I was in the next room. Your boys, Lord. You made them watch," she hisses the word watch.

"They're liars. Probably faggots, too."

He looks out the window, clicking his tongue against the backside of his teeth. His eyes quote the moonlight, but lack their own sheen. Then he places the gun on the chest and unbuckles his belt. The clasp gives little bell rings as it strikes the latch. He lifts his shirt over his head. He lowers his zipper and kicks off his boots.

"Get in the bed."

She takes a mind to run, but her legs and arms grow heavy. Whippings and hard fucking had been separate tortures till now, but she knew someday they'd meet. Still palming the pistol, he mounts her and presses his right hand over her lips.

He raises her hem. His penis stiffens against her thigh, slick with another woman's juices, not long ago removed from her own daughter's sex. Nauseating.

He thinks they're making love, and the worst part's that in his tangled mind he's teaching her a lesson. Each time she squirms or cries out he raises the pistol to her temple. She fights tears long as she can, but when she feels him quicken and his lower body tense, she weeps. He places the pistol flat against her forehead and moves his hips faster, pounding her pelvis. Every thrust drives more breath from her lungs. Little shards of broken soul ride the gasps, lost forever to the air.

When he comes, his finger curls around the trigger. The pop bursts in her ears, and something hot and horrible sears her scalp. At first she thinks he's shot her in the head; but he rolls off, muttering, cold gobs of semen frost her thighs, and the odor of gunpowder and singed hair fill her nostrils.

When she wakes he's gone, and she's empty, carved inside out, drained of spirit, blood, and juice. She rises and wanders room to room, finally entering the kitchen, unsure what she's after. Last night was the last time he'd have his way—of that much, she's certain.

She opens and closes the refrigerator, inspects empty cupboards, then opens the drawer with the scissors in it. She takes them from the drawer, slides her feet into a worn pair of athletic shoes, and steps onto the porch. She looks long at Black Rock Mountain, then raises the scissor points to her temple.

The blades don't slice; instead, they pull, bringing hateful pain. Her hair is thick and unruly as straw, tar black and streaked gray. The first lock yields to the dull blades and a ten-inch tuft drifts from her scalp to the ground. Another strand, then another, then another. A couple inches remain, and she fingers the frayed ends, combing it with her fingers to feel the burn on her scalp. A trench flows an inch from her hairline back. It's a brand.

Raindrops plummet fast and fat, rattling the porch roof like cavalry drums. They explode on the concrete path through the yard like little bombs, dousing the well's metal handle, drenching the howling dogs, soaking the driveway gravel, filling depressions with miniature lakes and rivers.

The scissors slide from her fingers; they fall end over end, landing in hair and dirt. She ambles from the porch into the yard. The earth sucks at her soles with each step, pulling her back and down on her heels. He left the gate ajar. Holding the hinge-side post, she pulls through it. Her mud-slathered shoes must weigh ten pounds each.

A railroad crossing divides the road. The tracks slice Ebb Holler, dividing livable areas from mountain slopes, settled areas from wild, good folk from black-Dutch. The tracks lay a steel border between what passes for living and what's mere survival. She crosses the tracks rarely, usually only to gather herbs, attend service, or visit the dead, whose scattered graves honeycomb the holler. The path up Black Rock Mountain begins on the other side.

She leaves the gravel, mud again, legs drawn down again. Her calves burn. She struggles to raise each leg. Little brown streams gurgle down the channel slicing the path's center between her legs, carrying loess in their flow. The dirt in the water smells clean and real. Boughs wring and writhe above, twisting into a ceiling.

She walks out of her shoe. She grabs hold of a skinny birch trunk, and a knot in the bark cuts the webbing between her second and third fingers. Rocks beneath the flowing water slice her foot calluses. Pain pulses, keeping time to her heartbeat. She pushes a bloody foot back into the shoe and continues up the hill.

At the overgrown cemetery cut into the woods just off the path, she sits on a stump beside a tiny rock with the letters *S. H.* cut into on it. Her father, Serious Hampton, lies beneath. She hums for a little while, rocking back and forth to the rhythm of her own voice, then settles into silence. She removes her shoes and lets the water coursing down the mountain wash her toes. Clean feet and hands are a luxury.

Through a stand of maple trees into the holler, she glimpses the swollen river, colored the brown of over creamed coffee. Captained by a black, shaggy-haired hound, a single-wide floats down the river sideways. The dog looks scared. Lightning in the distance; ten seconds later, thunder. She counts off the seconds and the miles. There's more coming.

"You was right, Daddy. Oh, Lord. Can't you tell me where they took the baby?" She laughs at herself for half expecting an answer, thankful there's no one here to see her. But she's unable to help herself: "Tell me, please?"

She falls into the mud and digs at her father's marker with bare hands, clawing its edges. But she gets nowhere—the marker's a lie, like everything else. Not a disk lain flat, but a long concrete cylinder sunk longways. She concentrates on the dirt directly before it, alternately scooping handfuls of wet earth and pounding it flat with fists.

She shrieks into the rain and wind, desperate to bring to the surface the last man she'd known who carried sweetness in his soul. Gobs of mud cake her fingers, her knees slip, and she falls flat on her stomach. Each time she falls, she brings herself back to kneeling and digging like a hound, flinging the earth behind.

She thinks at first that she's slipping again when the earth shifts, but she's overcome with the sensation of movement, and then she knows the very ground between her knees is tumbling down the mountainside. Two centuries' worth of mining, burials, clear-cuts, strip mining, plantings, buildings, burnings, gales, and storms, and the mudslide's overdue, but she can't help but think she's helped bring it about.

Perhaps the last tear to slide from her nose was the final gram the old peak could take before bucking her off. The idea embraces her, and she savors the feeling of control. Didn't Jesus say you could move a mountain?

The slide gathers strength, and the ground opens in a deep red groove, and water rushes from everywhere on the mountain to fill it; the trench becomes a river and it tows her, pulling her down the path. From behind comes the sound of cracking wood; just then she pays the sound no mind, sure it's a complaint from saplings uprooted in shifting soil.

That's before she turns to the sight of a rotten pine box—long yellow finger bones hanging from a split in one side, and Serious Hampton's skull laughing through the half-off lid. She welcomes the company. To be alone and in such a shape's a pickle sure enough. She reaches for the box. Not a doubt in her mind it'll carry her to safety; without it, she'll slip under, and once below, she'll never rise again.

SISSYNECK

LEXINGTON 2000

Kyle has studied Mr. Jackson's habits. Out by 6:00 a.m., in by 2:00 p.m. He always says good morning or good afternoon to the staff; he's so careful about referring to the time of day properly that once, during a midday return to retrieve a deposition transcript, he wished the bellman good-noon. On Fridays he leaves a ten dollar bill on the bed that Kyle takes as a gesture of appreciation for keeping the room clean.

Mr. Jackson carries a soft brown briefcase. The girls at the desk say he's a big-shot lawyer. He has more shoes than someone with mostly neutral colored suits has a right to, and he lines them up in ordered rows on the floor and the closet's top shelf: browns of subtle, varying shades; blacks with and without buckles; slip-ons; lace-ups, all shined. Grey, black, and deep purple suits crowd the rod, their jacket shoulders so wide they abut the closet door.

Kyle draws his cart into Mr. Jackson's room. It's not the only room he's used in the past couple of weeks, but it's his favorite. There's an exotic quality to the scent here, a mix of musk and toiletries hinting at Mr. Jackson's meticulous grooming. Kyle likes to think Mr. Big-Shot Attorney takes great care each morning to sculpt himself into a likeness of the confidence that defines him.

He sits at the foot of the king-sized bed, atop a floral patterned comforter. All the beds on this floor have the same dreadful, busy bedspread, in a print that Minnie Pearl might have worn. The rooms themselves are no better, no newer. Maple furniture, bronze fixtures, bronze trim. Underfoot pale green carpet spans wall to wall, dotted with little red diamonds, good for hiding spills and stains. Rustic watercolors hang on the walls. Furniture, carpet, bedspreads, paintings— all diluted pastels. Spring without end, Amen.

Kyle unlaces his black boots and removes them. He leans back, unbuttons his black canvas pants and slides them down. He flexes his ankles. The pants drop in a heap at the foot of the bed. He grabs the neck of his white polo and pulls it off. Socks next, then T-shirt. He drops his underwear to his feet, then takes a towel and a small green bottle of multi-purpose gel from the service cart. Just the things a boy needs to get clean.

In the bathroom, Kyle leans into the shower and turns the water on; a stream patters the tub, flicking at the edge of the shower curtain. He yanks the curtain across the tub to let the steam build. His pink silhouette moves in the misted glass: a ghost. Plastic tubes and bottles litter the countertop around the porcelain washbasin—a tin of pomade, Crest, Old Spice, Tend-Skin with aloe for shaving bumps, baby oil.

After three long days without a shower, Kyle's ripe. He can smell himself—an odor of fried bologna sprinkled with brown sugar and plain old ass. The crust of half a week's work is hard on his skin; his hair is slathered to his scalp like he's styled it with lard. Minuscule pieces of cotton from his socks, underwear, and T-shirts lodge between his toes, his buttocks, in his armpits—little balls of fabric, sticky with sweat, dried stiff from his body heat.

Kyle places the towel on the toilet lid but keeps the shower gel in hand. He moves the curtain and steps in. The water hits him below the navel. He wets his hair. Worth leaving Slocum County for water pressure alone. He steps back from the jet and squeezes the plastic gel bottle. The liquid oozes into his palm.

He rubs his hands over his body: face, chest, stomach, arms, underarms, genitals, legs, buttocks, the skin between his toes. He massages the shower gel into his scalp and steps into the stream again, letting the water beat his skull. The lather drains into his eyes, the wrinkles around his mouth, behind his ears. The pulsing, droning water quiets his mind. Good to be clean.

When Mr. Jackson sweeps the curtain aside, Kyle reels against the wall. He screams once, loud and short, like a frightened girl, then goes quiet, blinking at the giant lawyer through soap-soaked eyes. He holds out his hands to shield himself from a blow. But there is no strike. He cups his hands over his crotch.

"O God. I was—"

Mr. Jackson holds out the towel. "Here."

"I can't hardly see." Kyle takes the towel and presses it to his face.

"I can," says Mr. Jackson, crossing his arms. His stare traces Kyle's body. Kyle lowers the towel over his privates.

"I didn't mean no harm—"

Mr. Jackson's nod says he's expecting more in the way of an explanation. Kyle says nothing. Mr. Jackson turns the water off and instructs him to finish drying. He walks into the room, slamming the bathroom door. Kyle stands wet and pitiful, a drenched mutt. He dries, cinches the towel around his waist and steps from the tub. Deep breath, and he opens the bathroom door.

The room is freezing. Mr. Jackson sits at a table by the window, outlined in the light of midday, legs crossed at the knees. His wrist is bent backward, a menthol cigarette vertical between his index and middle fingers. White shirt open at the collar. Grey silk tie, loose knot. A silver blazer drapes his chair back.

"Sit," he says.

Kyle sits on the bed, facing Mr. Jackson. His clothes rest beside him on the bed, folded and stacked, shirt on socks, underwear on T-shirt, pants on underwear. Kyle touches the pile with his finger. "I'm sorry about using your shower, please don't tell nobody."

"What's your name?"

"Kyle Nash."

"Kyle Nash, why are you showering in my room?"

Kyle looks into his lap.

"I was getting ripe. I ain't showered in a few days."

"Your clothes could get up and walk by themselves."

Kyle reaches for his shirt. "Nice of you to fold them."

"I don't like messes—don't put those on. They need to be laundered."

"Ain't got nothing else to wear."

"Why not shower at your place?"

"Ain't got one."

"A friend's place."

"No friends, neither. Not here."

"An empty room?"

"Booked solid for two weeks."

Mr. Jackson pauses, takes a drag. "It has been busy. Kyle, your accent is pronounced. Where are you from?"

"Out east, near Virginia. Slocum County."

"What brings you to Lexington?"

There are so many reasons, all piled together, that they've become a big mess that's more feeling than justification. Kyle has no words for the feeling, and it floats over all his other thoughts like a storm cloud, complicated and nameless. "Ain't got slightest," Kyle admits.

Leaning out of the shadow, Mr. Jackson gestures at Kyle with the first two fingers of his right hand, like he's about to throw the cigarette across the room. He takes a breath, as if to speak, but instead of speaking, he stands and walks to the bureau. From the bureau, Mr. Jackson retrieves a red sweatshirt and a pair of blue soccer shorts. He throws them on the bed, then picks up the phone and leans against the bureau, twirling the phone cord around his finger. Kyle takes the clothes into the bathroom to change, but doesn't close the door. He removes the towel and hangs it over the curtain rod.

"This is two-seventeen. Send up two filets. I think green beans will be appropriate. Uh-huh. Bill it to the room. Can you connect me with the concierge? Thank you." Kyle hears him suck on the cigarette, then: "The tickets were fine, thank you. Can you do me a favor? I have some laundry. A pair of slacks and a shirt. Can you send someone? I've got room service coming. Kill two birds, perhaps? Yeah. That'd be great."

When Kyle returns, Mr. Jackson is at the table again. His clothes are too big for Kyle, but anything is better than prancing around in that towel.

"You may wear those until your things are laundered. I've ordered lunch."

"I couldn't eat with a guest. There's rules."

"Rules? Please. Sit."

Kyle sits. Mr. Jackson tamps his cigarette into an ashtray on the desk. "What's it like? Slocum County."

"You ain't been?" Mr. Jackson shakes his head; no, he hasn't. "Hills, mostly. I say it's pretty ugly—mountains pretty, people's ugly."

"I'm sure the people are lovely."

Kyle rubs his nose on the sleeve of the sweatshirt. "We lived up in Ebb Holler. I had a trailer. Ain't like you think. It was nice. Pathfinder doublewide. I got it after the flood. You can't tell it was sunk, except for a brown ring six feet up. Real faint. I thought it looked like a decorator border. Didn't even mold."

"Why leave?"

"I didn't get along." Kyle sucks his bottom lip under the top row of his teeth. "I'm not like them. I like to read, watch movies on the classics channel. Mr. Riddle let me splice his satellite dish. *On the Waterfront*, I liked that. Any them old movies. *Funny Face*—"

Mr. Jackson nods. "Audrey Hepburn."

"Gorgeous." The word dallies in Kyle's mouth. "I got books from the Slocum County library—Beats, Jesse Stuart, Faulkner—Ms. Blevins, the librarian, said I'm her best customer. That's what I am I guess."

"You work?"

"Daddy got killed in the mines. I got Social Security, but they cut it off at eighteen."

"Your mother?"

"Tonya had me after she got out of the reformatory. Took to oxys when I was in high school."

"You call your mother by her first name?"

"We're more like brother and sister."

"You finish school?"

Kyle shakes his head. "They called me names. Kicked out for fighting."

Mr. Jackson rises to a rap on the door. He motions for Kyle to hand him the dirty clothes. Mr. Jackson negotiates an exchange of food for soiled clothing. Kyle knows the voice; nervous, he crosses his arms and stares through the sheers at cars crawling Route 27.

Mr. Jackson brings a big tray of food. He returns to his place before the window and motions to the chair before the desk, telling Kyle to join him. The tray looks nice: two silver domes stretch across the plates and in the middle of the tray; two wine glasses beside an uncorked bottle of red wine. Kyle smells butter on the green beans and charcoal on the filet. Pangs grip his stomach, each a vise. For the first time since getting busted today, he remembers he hasn't eaten since yesterday. Mr. Jackson unrolls his napkin and uncovers his plate. Kyle uncovers his, too. He saws his steak.

"*Bon appétit*," Mr. Jackson says.

"Mine's got a toothpick in it."

"You can take that out."

Kyle points at the filet with his fork. Through a mouthful of green beans and steak he says: "Wrapped in bacon. That's neat."

"Wine?"

"That all we got? Then I'll have some."

He pours Kyle's glass half full, then fills his own.

"Mr. Jackson—"

"Marion. I insist."

"Don't seem right, but okay. Marion. Reckon you ain't telling?"

"Difficult fact pattern. You've been cleaning my room, with access to my things for two months. You know me better than some of my colleagues and clients, but we've never spoken at any length before now. You know what kind of deodorant I use. You know my schedule—don't you? I see you every morning as I depart. You know when I return. You never expected to get caught. You're always sincere. That's what I look for. Sincerity. Rare thing, that, truly, in a person. That and gentleness. You're sincere and gentle. You've not stolen from me, though you could have. You're friendly and honest. You leave the room spotless."

Marion's voice sounds like sap looks. Kyle blushes. He's not sure why. Marion shrugs, looking at Kyle over the rim of his wine glass.

"I've tried to leave a little token now and then. I was angry when I came back today. But, on reflection, you were using my shower for a good reason. Not having a shower of your own is a good reason to use someone else's."

"Been living in my Pontiac." Kyle says it before he can stop himself. "Ain't had a job long enough to rent an apartment."

Marion raises the napkin, covers his mouth, and clears his throat. "You sleep in your car?"

"It's near campus. Cops see me all curled up in the back seat think I'm sleeping off a drunk. Ain't bothered me yet. I move the car in the morning. I been pulling it off."

"You came here without money?"

"I had some."

Marion looks relieved.

"But it's all used up. I bought gas with it."

Strain returns to Marion's face.

"How long have you been at this?"

"Two months this coming Wednesday. I'm saving most of my checks. I'll be okay soon as I get first and last months rent."

Marion attends his steak. Kyle sips the wine. Grimace: his taste buds haggle with the hot-dry Cabernet. Marion seems concerned with something he can't, or won't, say. He cuts his green beans into successively smaller pieces. Kyle feels vulnerable, almost more than when he stood naked. Nobody knew about the car. He pushes a pallid sliver of fat around the plate with his knife.

"I grew up in Atlanta," Marion says.

"I seen the Olympics on my splice," Kyle says. "Atlanta looks nice. I ain't been."

"You never saw Tuxedo Park on your satellite."

Marion makes a cross of his cutlery, leans back, crosses his legs, and lights another cigarette. "I didn't fit in either. I didn't go for sports or gangs or hanging out on the corner. That didn't feel real. I'm big. Among my community we feel pressure to act a certain way. Everybody wants to know why you're not playing ball. People have expectations, and if you don't act to suit those expectations, people sometimes react in a negative way."

"My cousins and all them was most times up on Tuck's Branch, drinking, screwing, and smoking pot."

"You understand. I was intellectual, for one. My cousins called that acting white, but it is not. I liked music—not just hip-hop, though I enjoy it and there's a place for that. Classical, too, and jazz. Art—I used to ride a bus to the museum. Haunted the place. The guards and docents knew me. They knew my name. They'd say 'Hey, Big M.' I felt real when they did that. Someone knew me. You get it? Me. An aficionado, pee-wee expert on Kouros sculptures. They knew my habits. Not some idea stitched together from the misbehavior of boys they'd known."

"You feel like they're the only ones who know you. Like Mr. Riddle."

Marion takes a long drag. "Tuxedo Park? Pressure. There was a role they wanted me to take, but when I got alone I was real. Now, lying's a sin. They love that sin shit back in the country. I've got rural family myself. Crazy in the hell and sin scene, all of them; but the only thing I believe to be sin is dishonesty. It's a shame, too. The only way to survive when they hand you some role, to which you are unsuited, often as soon as you're born, is lie, lie, lie." Marion punctuates the repetition with chops at the table. "I got a scholarship. Kissed the brothers on that corner goodbye. Found places where Marion Jackson could be himself, not his mamma's baby or some big lazy brother thinking he was too good to ball. People like you, like me, must flee such environments. Even if you must drive across Kentucky, with no money, and sleep in your car. Otherwise we must continue to lie. Lying kills. It will kill you, Kyle."

Kyle feels like Marion's been in his mind, rifling through his thoughts and memories, like a lawyer rifling through a file drawer, locating Kyle's ineffable ideas and calling them by their names. Kyle stands, hands shaking. His knees are so weak that he must concentrate to keep from sitting again; he backs away.

"Thanks for the food," he says. "And for not telling."

"You're uncomfortable. I'm sorry. I didn't mean that. I think I know where you're coming from."

"You didn't," Kyle lies, grinning, and he laughs nervously, then points at the door. "I—they're probably downstairs, I didn't clock out. They'll think I took off with the cart."

Kyle offers his hand. Marion stands, clasps it gently. Kyle realizes he's still in Marion's clothes.

"Your clothes," he says.

Leaning across the table, Marion firms his grip and meets Kyle's lips. Kyle sees Marion's face moving toward his and he knows Marion's going to kiss him, but there's a disconnect between his eyes and mind, as if he were in his body but not controlling it. He's a guest in his own skin. Instead of avoiding the kiss and directing Marion toward his zipper, as he might have done in the dark behind the Slocum County Greyhound station, he lets Marion's mouth fasten wet, soft, and sweet, on his.

It's different, here in the light, with names exchanged and bodies and faces and hands in full view. This is not a desperate, frenzied coupling in an alley behind a dumpster; this is real and electric and alive. Kyle receives Marion's tongue for a moment, but as he does his chest heaves, trembling in lust and self-loathing. His penis thickens, but he presses his hand against Marion's chest, pushing him away. Kyle shakes his head and steps toward the door.

"You think you know me, but you don't. You don't know me."

"Kyle. Kyle, wait."

When Marion calls his name again, Kyle's so confused Marion might as well be calling from outside. He thumps barefoot down the hallway. The door slams behind him as he gathers speed. He knows how to run. The elevators at the end of the corridor rush to meet him, growing larger with each stride. Breathless, he presses the down button. It winks orange. A row of backlit numbers embedded in the stainless-steel cornice says the car is on the 18th floor. He needs motion, action, speed. He needs them. Needs them now.

Kyle presses the crash bar on the stairwell door. He descends the stairs two and three at a time, skipping more as his pulse quickens. He holds the banister loose, leaping one landing to another. At the first floor, he bursts through the emergency exit. Sirens wail. He gasps, filling his lungs with brisk autumn air.

Outside: Lexington as usual: numb white people in suits shuffling, their labors' futility camouflaged in smug self-importance. How can they move in this world, walking and talking but still asleep? Somewhere in this city hillbillies and lawyers are French-kissing, hopeless wives taking lovers, horny teenagers fumbling with one another's bodies, randy husbands dropping two hours' pay for a lap dance, and worse, oh worse, a million others are telling lies nobody believes about what and who they'll do and what and whom they won't.

Kyle runs faster—his long feet are calloused, and the concrete is kinder than gravel and the mountain mulch to which they're accustomed. He runs, weaving through the crowds as he meets them. There is no time to deal with them. They would run too, were they him.

The hotel recedes, the center city's buildings diminish. Trees dot the hills of the university neighborhood; wet, rotting leaves grind underfoot as he darts left, onto Leader. Cresting the hill, his nose fills with a smoky tease, calling to mind the overwhelming, jewel-toned autumn that, by now, will have overtaken the hills. Mountains fill his mind, low and rolling, old as fear, bowing to the season as it washes over, dappling hollows gold, red, and brown.

At his Pontiac he thinks for the tiniest moment to flee home to those hills. A dark, terrible place, familiar and comfortable all the same. But that thought vanishes as quickly as it comes. He leans over the roof of his Pontiac and rests his head on his arms. Sweat stings his eyes. He meant to sit in his car while catching his wind and ordering his mind, but the impulse to run on pulls him one way, while an urge to crawl into the Pontiac pulls him another. Neither is right.

Lies and false reasons and make-believe swirl around him like dithering leaves. Kyle decides he will not allow them to settle or pile up and cover this day, these truths, that kiss, not again, nevermore. He pounds the roof of the Pontiac with the side of his fist, and it rumbles like a timpani. He raises his head to light. No sense in fighting it. He will go back and knock on Marion's door. When it opens he will enter, and once inside, he will stay.

THE DONE THING

CHICAGOLAND 1977

Penny Mastropolous rolls South Side to collect Billy Nash, her brother, from the Harrison Street Greyhound Station. She pilots her barge of a Lincoln; new, Dimi bought it for her—seats tangerine leather, power everything, and an FM radio. Beautiful, beautiful, the soft color of warm margarine. She twists a cigarette into her black and gold cigarette holder and raises the Lincoln's lighter to the tip of her cigarette.

Chicago's not so different from Slocum County. Manmade terrain swells and declines just like God-pressed Appalachian earth, and to either side, mirror-windowed skyscrapers rise like cliff faces. Neon stripes the hood in abstract patterns. Farther south, buildings shorten and darken into windowless cubes corralled by rusty fences, topped with coils of concertina wire, unruly as sycamore limbs. Streetlights reveal the structures as she approaches. Signs everywhere, first dim, then headlight illuminated, dim again. Firetrap warehouses, tool & die shops, liquor stores, porno theaters. Distant tenements are mountains made of I-beams.

She parks behind the one story, redbrick Greyhound station. Three men wait below the corrugated steel canopy, like their counterparts down home, itching for mischief, except these here are darker and leaner, wearing unkempt afros instead of bent-billed ball caps, jiving instead of jawing; they terrorize a thin white security guard instead of pestering a docile black janitor. They howl. As she nears, their taunts more aggressive.

"Damn, you fine."

"Hold on, sweet thing, hold on."

"What's your name, baby?"

A large man with skin like varnished pine blocks her path. Penny removes the cigarette holder from her mouth and gestures to the guard. Penny crosses her arms.

"Aren't you supposed to do something?"

He looks at his shoes. The big man licks his lips. His comrades guffaw, mouths hidden behind fists.

"How you doing?"

"Get your ass out of my way and I will be just fine."

"Where's your man? I'll be your man."

"My man? You mean Dimitri Mastropolous? My husband?" Penny takes a drag, then blows smoke in the big man's face, which shifts in an instant from playful to concerned. The men behind roar, though grimacing. The thought of the big man's chest, gone suddenly ice water cold, pleases her.

"You lying."

"My name is Mrs. Penny Mastropolous. Now, you going to get the fuck out of my way or shall I have your legs broken? One phone call."

No doubt he is trying to decide how to wiggle out of this

while saving face with his friends. Finally he steps aside. She flicks ash at the cowed security guard in passing.

Inside, gnarly cigarette filters litter the floor. Confused people mill about, as if KO'd by fluorescent light. Some talk to themselves, others look angry, the remainder look sleepy. Near a ticket counter, an old black man wearing a Kangol hat smokes a mint cheroot and holds court with a custodian and an off-duty driver.

She finds Billy in a molded plastic chair that has a small coin-operated television attached to the armrest. A single speaker plays a crowd in high treble—they cheer generic jazz; a late night talk show, probably. She has not seen Billy in years, but he looks just like he did when he was little.

He wears a Cincinnati Reds baseball cap pulled down over his eyes. His work boots rest on a green army duffel, probably one of Junior's from Vietnam. A tinge of pity and embarrassment strikes her. Small but real, the sting of a sweat bee.

"Billy?"

He raises his head, eyes bloodshot. He stands and she hugs him, but she smells the booze on his skin and releases him earlier than etiquette says she should. He is tall and slim, healthy looking, wide in the hips and shoulders, big in the feet, like all the Nashes. He has two days of beard on his jaw, bristly black and grey.

"Your bus early?"

"My ride's late."

She points at his bag. "That it?"

"Travel light. Never know when you'll have to split."

She lifts his bag, then says, "You can never tell what tomorrow will bring."

"Sounds like a song."

They walk abreast. She sees her own features in Billy's face. The mountain lilt in her own voice, which, for five years, she's worked hard to contain, mainly by eschewing contractions, is absolute in his. Outside, the small-timers stand in nearly the same place, but a little closer to the guard, inquiring as to his mother's sexual proclivities. As Billy and Penny pass, the large man steps beside them, taking Penny's side. Billy stiffens—most Nash men figure they'll fight a black before saying hello to one.

"That's not Dimi Mastropolous," he says. "I know what Dimi look like. That ain't Dimi."

Penny switches the cigarette holder and Billy's duffel bag, hand to hand, hitting the big man in the shin.

"My brother. He works for Dimi."

A lie: Billy has come north, on no notice at all. He called from Indy that afternoon to say he was halfway there. Work had not entered into it, not yet. At the Lincoln's trunk, the big man asks if he can help load Billy's bag. Penny rolls her eyes and tells him no. Billy hangs back, coiled like a rattler. The big man picks up a piece of littered paper from the lot, then scribbles a number.

"Tell Dimi call me if he need something. I work cheap, hell. I got boys, boys with respect. Dimi Mastropolous? Yeah."

Penny folds the paper into thirds and slides it in her pocket. She puts Billy's bag in the trunk. They get in the car. The big man waves, thinking, no doubt, how much he loves his legs.

"Who was that?"

"Some jig. Started with me when I got here."

"Why didn't you say something?"

"I took care of it. What you on your ass about?"

He burrows his shoulder between the seat and the door and pulls the bill of his hat down again. Penny ashes her cigarette and cranes her neck to check for cars before merging. Billy has fallen asleep, mouth open, drooling.

This was not how she imagined his arrival. She knew her kin would come, eventually, out of fear, boredom, or need. But she imagined it in the daytime, for one, when Chicago's restaurants cloud the air with the wonderful aromas: curry and tomatoes, and chili peppers and sweet grease from pizzerias, whipping around the buildings and each other, mixing to a good, generic food smell—crowing, yes, this place is alive with people and culture and has airs for a reason.

She imagined them greeted with honking horns, stacked traffic, Lake Michigan's gulls bitchy and screeching, all lain over millions traipsing the sidewalks in tides of hair and clothes and skin. Now, that would have impressed a briar.

None of that in Southside twilight. She wants him to love the city's bigness as much as she does, to hold it up against the hills like she has, to judge the hills harshly; she wants him to step from one identity to another, joining her. Billy is not impressed. She remembers, unhappily, that not much impresses him, and not much ever did.

Penny leaves the radio off, listening instead to the tires roll across creases in the pavement and tubular rings from disturbed manhole covers. She drives toward Edgewater, hoping she beats Dimi home, and gets Billy settled before she has to explain. When they pull in the driveway, Billy wakes and demands to know who lives here. But he knows.

She sees through his eyes for a moment, teased by

presuppositions about homes, land, and wealth. Faux columns lifting the portico would remind him of pictures on the Graceland calendar Opal kept in the kitchen. The soft yellow lights dousing the facade would suggest one word: class. Brick construction, blue shutters. Paved driveway, landscaping. He has never seen to beat. She would bet on it.

"What do you think?"

He makes clear distinctions between each word, taking time to pronounce every letter clearly, mocking her pronunciation.

"I think you are trying to cover up your hill-bill-ee accent."

"Nonsense."

"Nonsense."

"Stop it."

"Stop it."

"Dimi will be home soon. Let me talk to him first."

"Good. Finally get to meet my brother-in-law."

"He is in a bad mood sometimes. Usually. Keep to yourself tonight."

"Hell, Penny. We're kin."

He gets his bag and they go inside. Penny shoos him down the hallway to a guest room. He takes his time, pausing to comment on the artwork and marble tile.

"How much this cost?"

From the corner of her eye, she sees headlights trace the foyer wall. She pushes Billy into the guest bedroom. She jogs to the foyer, smoothing her shirt. She hears Billy's footsteps in the hallway. A Latina in a leopard-print blazer and black polyester pants opens the front door.

Penny feels like she's swallowed something heavy. The woman is beautiful. She has a tight, globular afro, silver hoop earrings and Gringa makeup. Lips thick and red as a Valentine's day card. She has painted her eyelids smoky, glittery blue. Dimi stumbles in, out of breath, coked out of his mind. He holds his gut with one forearm. His indigo Oxford hangs untucked on one side. His salt and pepper hair spins off in coils and waves, like somebody put a beard on him upside down.

"Hey baby," the lady says.

"PePe, I want you meet—"

"Roberta."

"Roberta is, how you say? Good friend. I bring her so we all be a friend."

Penny crosses her arms. Billy enters, clutching three bottles of beer.

"I guess I need more beer," Billy says.

"What about this! What is this?" Dimi howls. "This a man in my house and I not at home! Pussy is the pussy, but a cock—" he makes a thrusting motion with his pelvis, "the cock, he go inside! This a man be inside my wife!"

"*Whoa.* Hold up now. I don't know what you heard about Kentucky, but—"

"Kentucky?"

"Hell yeah, brother."

"You a—the Nash?"

"Ain't *the* Nash. That's a lot to bear. I'm *a* Nash."

"Géneia! I worry! A man my house, I no home. Which of a you brother?"

"Billy."

"Penny no say you're coming. I no say the visit is yes."

Penny shakes her head and looks at the floor. When she raises her head, Roberta steps toward the door.

"Looks like the party's over," she says.

"There's never a party here for you," says Penny, pushing her out. "There's a Standard Oil on the corner, about a block that way," she points. "Call yourself a cab, slut." Penny slams the door so hard it rattles the frame. When she turns, Dimi's talking to Billy.

"Billy Nash, you eh—how you say? You will excuse?"

"I'm taking this beer."

"Take as many you want. You guest, a géneia."

Penny knows Dimi labors under some insincere bullshit Greek idea of hospitality, and knows further Billy can't tell the difference. He thinks Dimi is being polite from heart, not habit. Billy does not know, he does not fucking know. He cannot fathom. When Billy is gone Dimi hits her hard, in the teeth. Penny's lip bleeds. She tastes it; copper. He hits her again, left eye.

"Who you? I tell you bring somebody from Kentucky my house? One Kentucky bad enough, too bad, too hard for house train. This Kentucky don't have a tit or a pussy? No. Do he have the job?"

"Fuck you."

"He wait a cocktail in my bar like a sister? Suck me off after work?"

"He was halfway here when I learnt—learned—he was coming. He called from Indianapolis."

Dimi mocks her, sing-song: "He a call me from the Indianapolis."

Again. He hits her in the same place, every time, trying to shine her eye. If it does not look like her eye is blackening, he hits her again. He likes results.

"Chicago need more the white trash. You beg me to breathe, mouni."

Knees on marble, she covers her face like a cornered boxer. He jerks his pants at the waist and spits in her face, leaving her curled up beneath the tiffany chandelier.

"One week," Dimi says, mounting the stairs. "One." He pauses, midway up the flight. "I have a limit the patience, PePe. Don't fuck Dimi. I take you back I find you. I will do it." He sweeps his arm across the foyer, wiping everything in front of him away. "This? Poof."

She cries but not so much she can't turn it off and compose herself to deny him the satisfaction of having hurt her. Black eyes? She'll put up with one or two. Crying won't do—means they broke you. She'll take a dozen black eyes before she'll let him see a tear. One eye has swollen nearly shut.

"Didn't tell him I was coming?"

Penny uncovers her face. Billy stands in the hallway shadows, shirtless, beer bottle against his hip. Unsure how to take his tone; she searches his face for compassion with her good eye. She searches, and searches.

"Hell, Penn. You got to keep a man informed."

The guest room door slams shut. The door to the master suite opens.

"PePe! You a come to bed!"

For the rest of the week, she deals with two Dimis. Billy's in the room and Dimi salaams and fawns like Billy's Aristotle Onassis. Billy makes dumb parallels between Mediterranean and Appalachian hospitalities. She cooks and cleans and smokes, more disgusted by the moment with Dimi's insincerity, and Billy's simplicity.

Penny takes Billy to the city on Friday. She wears her largest sunglasses and darkest lipstick. They walk the grid, hands in pockets, hair waving in the sea breeze. She shows him the Civic Center Picasso, pointing with her cigarette holder like a docent.

"Picasso," she says, staring into the twisted brown steel. "Heard of him?"

"It's a piece of shit. Looks like one them monkeys with big blue noses."

"I am trying to show you the city."

"Bunch of Pollacks. Sorry to ruin the tour, ma'am, but I been to Toledo. I seen a city. Suppose I should've made a reservation."

They have lunch at the gaudiest Chinese restaurant Penny knows. The one with faux-gold-leaf paint on the walls, fake jade plastered on every surface. Sulking gods, big-bellied Buddhas, and stylized chows perch in a riot of color and geometry, hidden like spies.

Billy makes cracks about puppies and kittens served in mucus, but he cleans his plate and guzzles four beers. Penny worries it's only going to get worse: Billy, continuing to misinterpret Dimi's forced friendliness, will overstay his welcome, and Dimi will toss him out on the street, and her in Cook County Family Court, with a dime-store lawyer at her side, no money in her pocket, and an accent back in her mouth, thick and bitter, like a swallow of castor oil.

Billy lances a piece of breaded chicken from her plate with his chopstick. He leans back. In that posture, she sees he's developed a little potbelly, round and perfect as a medicine ball, like the Old Man's.

"You want me to help you look for a job?"

"How about I worry 'bout me, and you worry about you?"

"I just want to know what your intentions are."

"I intend not to go to jail."

"You're in trouble."

"You're better off not knowing. Listen. About your old man. Sounds to me like you made a better waitress than a wife. He ain't so bad. He is a ticket, ain't he? Guess you saw that right off. You're a hillbilly—stop trying to act different. I may sound dumb, but you sound dumber'n me, got your jaw clenched up, like they talk up here. You act a fool. You act a fool, somebody's gonna hit you."

Her black eye, healing, still safe behind the shades, throbs, and the cut on her lip burns. She shakes her head, astounded he can see everything so clearly and understand not a bit of it. She thinks of Kentucky and the Old Man, all that mess, and then remembers a queer confidence in her ability to spot darkness, and wrong, and call them by their names.

"You're right, Billy. I am very, very embarrassed."

That night Dimi dances playfully around the kitchen's island counter. "Billy, you a—you know how, how you say?" He punches at the air around Billy's face like Sugar Ray Robinson, ducking and weaving, jabbing, upper cutting. His gut hangs over his waist like a boil. His weight didn't bother Penny, but now it disgusts her. Billy looks out the back door, picking his teeth.

"Hell you on about? Fighting?"

"You the tough guy?"

"Hell. Had to be, growing up with her."

Penny does not laugh, partly because they expect her to, partly because he's being ironical, and irony is a luxury she does not feel entitled to yet. She rearranges some cookware in the sink, sure to bang the pans, as she knows that particular racket bothers Dimi, whose mother, when angry, banged pans while washing dishes.

"So you make use. You go with me and get some what they owe, the people." Dimi gestures southward. "You a big and look mean. You come? I pay." Penny rubs scrambled egg from the bottom of a skillet with an SOS pad. "Settle then," says Dimi. "You will go tonight a me and stand to look mean on my shoulder and make the people give the money. PePe! This one, he no so useless." He disappears into the hallway.

"Looks like I got me a job, sis."

"Birds of a feather."

Billy draws his fist. A familiar movement—an arm retracted, wrist on the end of a fisted hand, pulled back to the shoulder, a stretched rubber band, ready to spring and collide with a head or back or stomach and send a bitter wave of pain. His damnable posture multiples to a dozen in the stainless-steel pots, stovetop, and sink-bottom. Twelve of him, preparing to strike. She steps back, hands white with suds.

"Don't test me."

"That ain't—that's not—funny."

She has everything she ever wanted, and with it everything she didn't—a little Old Man, with a swollen, insistent penis, swaggering, clinch-fisted; a brother, his humanity dissolved in alcohol and coal dust, in front of her to remind of what she left behind. Billy struts out. Penny finishes the dishes in silence.

When Dimi comes downstairs, she is on the phone. He has wound up his hair in a towel like a diva. His pecs sag over his ribcage, puffed and effeminate. He carries a small scissors.

"PePe!"

She covers the handset with her palm.

"Who that? The boyfriend?"

"Telemarketer."

"What they sell? I no hear the bell."

"You were showering."

"Hang up now for trim the nose hair."

She hangs up and tends Dimi's nose hair. She asks him if he wants her to hem his pants or help with his makeup. Tough job being a tough Greek, she says. He laughs but she does not. She was not joking. Nobody understands anybody. It makes her want to scream.

At midnight, she waits on the bottom stair in her silk kimono robe. When the car arrives, she stands, walks to the door, and opens it after a single knock. Two stout Chicago cops stand on the stoop. She pulls her nightgown together at the neck.

"Ms. Mastropolous? Sorry to bother you at this hour. I regret—this may be difficult; would you like to sit? No? Very well. Ma'am, I'm afraid your husband may have been among a group of people trapped in a fire, near Woodlawn."

Penny slumps against the jamb, just like she practiced.

"My brother—he was with Dimi. Did he—was he?"

"There were some bodies without ID. Come with us?"

"Billy—he wore a ball cap. Big man, about yea—this tall."

They look at each other, then back to Penny.

"We can't be sure, ma'am. We'll wait while you ready yourself."

Before she climbs the steps to the bedroom that holds that wonderful closet filled with clothes from the Magnificent

Mile, she remembers to get the paper with the red ink phone number on it from beside the telephone, the number given her by the big man with skin like varnished pine, and she tears it to shreds. It would never do to have it found by the phone.

She ascends, debating the appropriate thing for a widow to wear. At the landing, she decides on black. It's the done thing. She has just the top and pants.

Interlude at a Rather Low Order

Outside Rimini 1995

A week ago Junie's story would've been an epic blame song: stanza after stanza on the Jews and niggers. But fact framed a newborn story in memories of a trip he took with the Old Man to Black Rock Mountain, thirty years back, at dusk on an autumn night, when they walked a winding trail for what seemed like miles.

Eventually, they came to a deep quiet place in the holler's bowels, confined on three sides by granite mountainsides and darkened by fawning branches. Junie thinks he heard falling water, but he can't be sure. The Old Man lugged a wriggling naked baby under his arm like a poke of taters. The baby's left arm, so much smaller than its right, was drawn up to its chest. It had no dimple under its nose, and its head was shaped like a watermelon.

It did not cry. It had never cried that Junie knew. It did not even cry when they left it to die, prone on a flat grey boulder.

This vernal morning, Junie sits on a red pleather stool at the far end of the bar at the Back Pass, tending his daughter and eating breakfast: scrambled eggs topped in cheese and ketchup, a side of home fries, coffee. His girl rests on the counter, mewling, swaddled in a fleece blanket.

He used to keep the blanket behind the truck's bench seat— for emergencies, back when emergencies seemed like good things to anticipate—before he recognized, by definition, bad surprises, impossible to anticipate. Shocks, to be endured.

The cook's hair hangs long; he wears shorts, a tie-dyed Grateful Dead T-shirt, and a long, grease-splattered apron. He paces the counter like some fascist dictator reviewing troops. In place of a riding crop, the spatula; in place of troops, the settings.

If the menus are out of order, the ketchup bottles less than full, or silverware detergent spotted, he makes a big production out of rearranging, refilling, or wiping down. Junie hopes he'll stop inspection before reaching the counter's end, where he will surely attempt small talk. It's almost four a.m., the cook is lonely, and the surest way to get someone to talk to you is hoping they won't. The cook wipes his fleshy palms on his apron. He's over-friendly in the way of a man who doesn't want you to rob him.

"How are the eggs? They're good?"

"Runny." Junie places his fork on the counter and wipes the corners of his mouth with a napkin. He stares the cook in the eye, rubs his stubbly scalp, and crosses his ankles. The cook can't see from his vantage, but Junie still wants to hide his red bootlaces.

"Don't see too many you fellas in here."

Junie rolls his eyes parallel to his forehead, giving his best impression of an angry bull ready to charge, and orders more coffee. The cook fetches the pot. The baby coughs. Junie thinks of the road. The cook returns with a steam-breathing pot and refills Junie's mug. Junie asks for milk.

"That's your daughter? Don't see too many of you fellas with babies. Let's have a look." The cook reaches for the blanket.

"I wouldn't," Junie warns. "If I was you."

The cook withdraws his hand, like he's touched a hot stove burner.

"Fine. He doesn't want me to see the baby. Fine."

Junie reaches into a baby blue diaper bag on the floor.

"Got a bottle for it here. Warm the milk."

The cook takes the bottle. He's dodged a bullet and he knows it.

"Why not? We're not busy."

Six weeks ago, the UPS guy left a corrugated cardboard box from Denmark at the guard hut. Junie was glad not to have been on duty. He hated dealing with UPS because the UPS guy always had a look on his face when he came to Wolfskamp gate that let you know, right off, he'd rather be delivering boxes full of warm sputum to a leper colony than dealing with skinheads.

Junie retrieved the box and lugged it to the cabin. His woman, excited and—he figured—hormonal, jerked the box from his hands the instant he arrived. She sat on a cane-bottom chair and tore into the box. She slashed at the edges with Junie's long-blade hunting knife, chattering as she worked. She was barefoot. He loved that.

She opened the box flaps and thrust both hands deep into the tricolor plastic popcorn, fishing for anything to grasp. Junie lit a cigarette and rubbed his belly. She raised a plastic bottle, holding it a few inches from her nose for inspection.

"Our baby will drink from this, Junie. Our baby."

Junie parked the cigarette in his mouth, tore the bottle from her hand and turned it over to see the markings on the bottle's bottom. He fumed.

"Made in Taiwan. Fucking bastards."

He aimed the brand at her nose. Her shoulders slumped.

"That ain't what the advertisement said."

"No it ain't. What should we do?"

"Call them. Get a refund."

"On an international money order?"

She tugged his elbow.

"Call, Junie. Call."

"I'm too pissed. I'll call tomorrow."

"You'll forget. Do it now. The cell's on the counter."

She clasped her hands and rested them on her belly. He paced, gearing up for the confrontation with the Danish baby supply people. There were times, such as this, when the cabin unnerved him greatly. It was so use-oriented, constructed for shelter and basic needs and nothing else, like the old house in Ebb Holler: not a right angle in the place. Particleboard walls, unfinished. Exposed wiring. Tin roof. Here, approaching the millennium, he still wiped his ass in an outhouse. Dust and odor everywhere, disorder spilling from within, to the threshold, out the door, into the yard. Beer cans, cigarette butts, used napkins, paper towel rolls, green bulb-shaped trash bags, full, ripped open by 'coons and possums after a snack. He'd fled to exactly the same place he'd fled from.

He stuffed his hands into the pockets of his black dungarees, removed his hands, then stuffed them back inside again. He took a final drag from his cigarette and extinguished it under his boot heel.

The counter lay in mounds of clutter, each unrelated to the pile nearest: a tub of muscle-building creatine monohydrate, a sheaf of notebook paper, vitamins and folic acid, stacks of resistance literature, a plate dotted with dollops of dried salsa and a fork. Over there, a box of pens. At the far end, the cellphone and charger cradle, plugged in the wall, the lights on both blinking "go" green. He pulled the phone from the charger.

"What's that number?"

She unfolded the packing slip. She traced a line low on the paper.

"Ask for Rasmus. He speaks English. Says it right here."

Junie jabbed the numbers into the keypad and lifted the phone to his ear. The futuristic ring in the cell's earpiece offended him. A woman's voice—lilting, kind.

"Hallo, International Hvid Spaedbarn-Stof."

"I want Rasmus."

The woman screamed for Rasmus in a stern Wagnerian voice very different from the one with which she'd answered the phone. The line went silent. After a moment, a man came on.

"Ja."

"This is Junie Nash, from America."

"Heil Hitler!"

"Heil Hitler. Listen, the paper said to call if we had a problem. That you spoke English."

"Ja."

"Your ad—hold on."

Junie dashed to the counter and retrieved a copy of *World Creator Monthly*, rustling through the yellowing newsprint until he saw International Hvid Spaedbarn-Stof's ad.

"Okay, your ad here says, and I'm quoting, that 'NONE OF BABY'S THINGS WILL HAVE BEEN MANUFACTURED

BY NON-ARYANS. REST ASSURED ONLY CLEAN WHITE HANDS WILL HAVE TOUCHED BABY'S THINGS.' We just unpacked the things and the baby's bottles were made in Taiwan. I'm not resting assured."

"This is why?"

"Taiwan? I don't study there's too many white folks working in a Taiwan baby bottle factory. You?"

"Don't worry, Mr. Nash. The bottles were made here in Denmark by good white people. I oversee them. We bought the molds used from a Taiwanese company. I sanitized them myself. Had them—how do you say it in English—sandblasted? Not to worry. Is there anything else?"

"I don't think I believe you."

"Well, why not? It's a perfectly fine explanation."

"I think we want our money back."

Rasmus pleaded half-seriously, condescending as only a European can, to an American. Junie could tell he was smiling.

"Mr. Nash, be reasonable."

"You be reasonable! Your ad says, 'ONE HUNDRED PERCENT SATISFACTION GUARANTEED, OR YOUR MONEY BACK.' I'm not satisfied."

"I'm sorry. It's too complicated to refund and change currencies and I'm afraid you're abusing goodwill by not believing my well-thought-out explanation even when it directly addresses your concerns."

"You're a bunch of damn liars." Heartbeat up, blood pumping, voice raised. "A bunch of Jews, too."

"You're the Jew, worrying after your money when your baby's bottles are fine and good and not made from Chinese people."

"I'll spread the word. You'll lose your American business. Fuck you," Junie seethed.

He threw the phone against the wall. He carried the confrontation for days. Something about it sat ill, deep and dim and formless. Perhaps it was the juvenile way they'd parted, slapping each other with the word Jew. He felt like a kid who'd lost a game of tag.

The cook returns with warm milk. Junie turns it over, squeezing the tiniest white droplet onto the webbing between his thumb and index finger. Mama did that for all four of his younger brothers: Liney and Cory and Wayne, and that one, the little baby with the drawn up arm, who lingers unnamed at memory's edge.

Warm enough, the milk; not too hot, perfect for the baby's mouth. Junie lifts his daughter and folds the blanket back, enough to expose her head. The cook angles, trying to peek, but from where the cook stands, he won't see a thing but a wriggling blanket and an upturned bottle.

"You want anything else?"

"No."

"Where are you from?"

"You know."

"Who's from there? Nobody. You're not from there. That's a place you end up, that place. Where did you grow up?"

"Kentucky."

"I have family there."

"Napkin."

The cook grabs a napkin from the perfect place setting next to Junie.

"Here, here. Take this. Babies are messy. I remember mine.

Little machines, those boys. I almost changed their names to spit, poo, and cry."

Junie dabs his daughter's upper lip with the napkin. Head lodged between Junie's triceps and forearm, she slurps, eyes shut, lips unsealed around the nipple, drawing milk the best she can. He did not realize how muscled and hard he had become over these last two years until something this small, tender, soft, and alive pressed against his muscles.

He loves her. She is the first thing he ever loved. He promised a thousand times to die for the aim of the Fourteen Words sacred to Klan and skinheads and Aryans and Creators and racists and bigots everywhere: *We must secure the existence of white people and a future for white children.*

Junie is at once free and bound by one truth, not dissimilar to the fourteen words, but more innocent: he would die for the existence of one white person, one white child, this one, lying in his arms, unaware of the tumult into which she was born.

"I have a cousin in Lexington. I visited three years ago."

The cook pulls up a stool and drops his massy bottom upon it. He rests his cheek in his palm and points the spatula at Junie.

"I was looking forward to some southern cooking. The food? Not so good. Chain restaurants, everywhere! The people were nice enough. I'll tell you: seems like independent-minded people gravitate south and west. That's why I came out, for college, from Chicago. I felt claustrophobic there, all the hustle and noise. But here—out here, oy. The land and spirit match up right. We got a lot of space, that's one thing. You can get away if there's something you don't like. You can live and let live."

The midwives lay the baby on a white metal table and looked at her in loathing, as if his daughter were made of dung. The head midwife removed her latex gloves and tossed them in the trash. The other did the same. They were finished.

Junie couldn't see the baby from where he sat, five feet or so from the table, because he'd dimmed the interior lights at his woman's request. She said the light hurt her eyes.

"What's the matter?"

Something was terribly wrong. The head midwife pretended not to hear. She reached for the doorknob. He rose, pulled the cigarette from his mouth, and blew smoke through his nostrils. He wanted to meet their eyes, to steal some clue, a warning about what to expect, but they wouldn't look at him.

The other midwife folded the SS battle flag in a perfect red square—the august and aged Alban Pontiff had blessed it, and they planned to wrap the baby with it. The midwives left. Nude and exhausted in the cane-bottom chair, Junie's woman said for him to come and dab the sweat from her head: it was in her eyes and it stung. She wanted to know why the midwives left and where the baby was. Her head lilted to one side—they'd dosed her with black-market morphine. Then the baby turned her head to Junie.

When he saw the harelip, he forgot to breathe. His woman dragged her forearm across her brow.

"What's wrong? I'm thirsty, Junie. Can't you get me some water?"

Junie poured some water in a red plastic Solo cup. The baby quieted, perhaps sensing his presence. Up close the harelip looked worse: The cleft rose from the left-center of the upper lip into the left nostril. It was rimmed in exposed fuchsia tissue, and slathered in mucus, spit, and snot.

His hand trembled. Lukewarm water spilled over the cup's rim, into the crevice between his thumb and forefinger. His woman's eyes were still shut tight and wrinkled at the corners like when she was in labor. Junie gulped his next breath like a man surfacing after a high dive into deep water.

"Baby's hare-lipped."

"No. It's not." She shook her head and flashed him a spacey grin. "You're crazy. Now 'bout that water?"

He put the cup to her bottom lip. She parted her cracked lips. Her breath blew hot on his hand. Junie tilted the cup and poured water on her tongue. She drank greedily and he raised the angle of the cup at her mouth until it was upside-down. Swallowing seemed unnecessary; her body absorbed the water before it reached her throat. Sated, she licked her lips.

"Now what's the matter, Junie? Where'd they go?"

Junie pulled a terrycloth towel from beneath the table. He wiped the baby's head and torso with the towel, and then swabbed the baby's limbs. Arms and hands, then legs, feet, little toes. He held the baby close to her face. It was almost an accusation. His woman narrowed her eyes and slouched forward; her breath was coming in thick rasps now.

"That's not my baby. Stop joking."

Junie heard a weird noise, like a stomach grumbling. She said she felt like she was having another baby and scooted to the edge of the chair. Blood and goop and what appeared to be a clump of black gelatin fell to the floor.

"Afterbirth," she said.

Junie wrapped the baby in another towel. She squawked again, ready to bawl, but he put the tip of his pinkie finger in her mouth: the baby sucked and seemed satisfied. He paced. His woman's head sagged. Still stoned, she didn't acknowledge him, or the baby. The baby had a long forehead and pronounced chin—all Nash.

His woman erupted, wailing; he spun. Her face twisted up and she clutched her stomach like it was splitting open and she was holding her guts inside. She tumbled from the chair, and came to rest on her back, her distended belly purpling. He felt sick and guilty because he hadn't noticed sooner. He thought they were shadows. Her thighs, bloody. He knelt and reached for his woman. She didn't seem to see him. She extended her hand.

"Junie? Junie?"

"Hold on, baby. I'm going to get somebody. Oh shit. Hold on."

"It's so dark."

He started to the door, but stopped when she gave a sound he'd never heard before; terrible, crunchy, like cracking rotten wood, followed by a whistling, wispy breath. Then her neck went slack; then, only silence.

Everyone has some excuse as to why he's where he is instead of where he means to be. Now his story has bent into itself, twisting, some threads unwound, others newly knotted.

He raises the baby to his left shoulder and pats her back while the cook sums his own excuses for being somewhere other than where he meant to be, explaining he did not intend to be forty-something, working in a diner on the edge of the world.

"I took a hit off a joint back in 1979, back when reefer was reefer. I was in law school, Berkeley. I took a semester off, went on tour, saw some Dead shows. What could go wrong?" He makes an open-armed, submissive gesture. "Next thing I know, I'm working here, George Herbert Fucking Bush is president, and I'm on the fat side of three hundred pounds.

I know by name every trucker running between Butte and Helena. Ten years gone, just like that." He snaps his fingers. "Borrowed money from Yaya, bought this place. Otherwise, I'd have been a complete failure. My mother, she tells people I'm a chef. How's that? Now they say that stuff isn't addictive, but I'm here to tell you something else. There was a time—if reefer had been free I wouldn't have worked. I don't do it any more, though." He winks. "Not much anyway. Maybe once a month. Or every few weeks."

"I like beer," Junie says.

"You fellas like the beer."

"There ain't no 'you fellas'. Not anymore."

The cook's eyes crawl his tattoos: the inverted swastikas, rounded edges of stylized 88's, jaws of skulls and the corners of flags of Scandinavian countries that bleed from Junie's neck hole and jacket sleeves. Junie removes the hand towel he'd placed over his shoulder and wipes the baby's chin. When the cook sees the baby's lip, he gasps.

"Problem?"

"No, no," the cook smiles. "Where's mommy?"

"Cremated her two weeks now."

"I'm sorry."

"You didn't know her."

"Sorry just the same. You're going to see the family?"

"*They* were our family."

"Some family. *Uh-unh.* Good for you, with the leaving. Nothing good comes from all that. Been people in here, asking questions—stank of FBI. We'll have another Waco, they don't watch. You take that baby on back to Kentucky. That's where you're going, isn't it? Home?"

Junie shrugs and rewraps the baby in the blanket. Fussy, but tired and full after having drunk half the bottle, she yawns and gives a halfhearted attempt at crying before she sleeps.

"I don't think we'll be going back."

"You could do worse than Kentucky. It seems a fine place to raise a child. My cousin's doing well. He owns part of a racehorse—knowing him, it's the ass end."

"I didn't turn out so good."

"You aren't dead yet."

"I don't feel exactly alive."

"They take something from you."

"It gets taken before they meet you. That's how they know you're theirs."

"Can I ask you a question?"

"Everything you've said has been a question."

"Has it? Oh, no. My father used to talk like that, always with the questions to questions. I've become my father." The cook collects himself. "How could you believe that stuff? That nonsense that the Jews want to take over the world? What did the Jews ever do to you? How many Jews could there be in Kentucky?"

"It goes like this," says Junie. "There's somebody in your life kicking you around. You're thinking no way, this shit ain't real, something's wrong; one day somebody whispers it's not your fault, you're not crazy. You been waiting to hear it forever. They fill that empty place with all their horseshit. It's the Jews. The ni—coloreds. They point out little things, have you watch the TV, count the Jew names."

"Jews control the media."

"Like *The Wizard of Oz*, when the dog pulls the drape back on the wizard."

"Jews producing, so you know."

"That's what I'm talking about. They get to you?"

The cook waves his spatula, laughing loud, as if the question holds subtle shades of humor Junie's missing.

"Not me. I don't let them near me if I can help it. I'm allergic to bullshit. So it goes from there. Jews control the media, Jews have the money, Jews want to control you?"

"Only thing stopping it's the will of the white race. Jews put the coloreds and the other mud people out to do their dirty work. To take us down." The baby farts. "Got a reason for anything you ask—Jews, Jews, always the Jews. You stop thinking of Jews like people. They get to be littler parts of a big thing that's not a lot of things apart, but hooked together, sharing secrets, working their plan."

"You had it sewn up! Why leave?"

"Had to get her away from that shit." Junie clears his throat. After a few seconds, he says, "Long drive comin'. I'll have the bill."

"What bill?"

"I got money."

"It's a gift. For the new you, the new her."

By noon, Junie and the baby are well into Idaho. He stands on the edge of a narrow gully cut by Spring Creek, burbling fifty feet below.

He holds his daughter close, rocking her, a father trying to keep a peaceful, sleeping baby quiet and sleeping. His red clip-on suspenders hang at his sides; he'd not bothered to lace his boots. He felt drunk from lack of sleep and shock and grief. The only thing keeping him tethered to the present is the baby, the baby, this little precious, helpless, girl.

In those drained and wasted moments, where for whatever small a time his weariness washed white-pride rhetoric from his mind, leaving a skeleton of reality, a shadow of a suggestion of how other people see, Junie realized half his attraction to this place and these people was geographical, the other half habit. Malcontent and mountain. It felt like home. He was angry and confused. His woman gone, a new woman in his arms; he felt unreasoned, animal, instinctual. Mourn and protect, keep moving. Keep moving, go west; it's how we run.

The Alban Pontiff's approach, slow and wending, broke his solitude. Junie turned, grateful, and greeted the aged leader. Junie seasoned his voice with respect and admiration, even a little fear. If anyone could arrange the shambles of Junie's life into order, it would be this man.

But the Alban Pontiff laid chaos, recommending infanticide. It would be better, the Alban Pontiff explained, that a deformed child should be put down than live among the fags, Jews, mud people, and race traitors when RAHOWA was finally fought and won. Then the old bastard turned away and shuffled down the path to the common areas of Wolfskamp.

Junie listened to the stream tumble over the rocks for a long time, dwelling not on Montana, but Kentucky, and babies, and secrets, and the gut-level human fear of deformity; about twisted minds who decide who dies and who lives.

He wondered how long it would take to get some things together. Making plans to run from where he'd run to, Junie held his daughter close, smelling the baby smell on her scalp, his lips pressed soft against her downy hair.

In time, the smooth sound of nature in course soothed his

frantic mind. *He would leave his daughter nowhere, he would take her everywhere, he would protect her. He would secure her existence, her future.*

SIMMER TILL YOU CAN'T STAND IT

KELLY'S BRANCH *2003*

Doyle adjusts his ball cap, squats, and clean-jerks my suitcase to his waist.

"Lift with the legs," he instructs, walking down the wooden steps and off the porch. "Not the back. You're not careful, you'll get you a hernia."

The front pocket of his bibs hold his glasses case and a rolled clutch of Redman. He spits amber in the weeds. A full key ring, fastened to his belt, tolls like sleigh bells.

"I studied it was you when I saw the name. We missed you last few years, but you didn't miss with us. I lost Aldene. That was last winter. A virus, best we can figure. They said get you a puppy, Doyle. I told them they ought to shit and fall back in it. Damn thing'd outlive me. Can't nary afford one since them yuppies in Lexington drove up the cost of a purebred bloodhound pup."

We follow a mulched path flanked on both sides by carefully arranged, whitewashed rocks. The trail winds halfway up the easy side of the mountain, to the same cabin I've rented for a summer week every year since I've been an adult, save the last few.

Doyle wants me to justify my absence, so I give him the short form version of my divorce, and explain that last year my son Hank was in the national finals of the President's National Physics Challenge, in Washington. I assure him I missed the river and his cabins. This raises his spirits.

"Sounds like you got a smart boy," he says.

Then he asks if I'm kin to the Slocum County Nashes. He asks me this every year, and every year I admit relation to whichever one of my aunts or uncles or cousins he's remembering. This year, he tells me it's a goddamn shame what Liney and that other boy did.

I agree, but caution him it's been over twenty years and things are always more complicated than the papers make them out to be. After a dozen silent steps, shuffling and leaning to one side to compensate for the weight of the suitcase, I feel the quiet, nervous guilt of a younger man watching an old man in labor, and offer to help.

"Let's say you be the guest and I'll be the hospitality provider," he calls over his shoulder. "That's what my lawyer calls me. Hospitality provider. Never heard to beat."

That evening, I smoke a Dunhill while watching the sunset explode between the porch posts, like frames in a series of framed photographs taken with filtered lenses—first: a fountain of orange, spat upward from the horizon, bursts over the hills; next, a Technicolor orgy tie-dyes the clouds, drawing all hues upward in vertical stripes before mixing them into deep cobalt; last: empty of color, a green canopy fades to charcoal.

Darkness comes complete, and I retire to the cabin. Doyle replaced the old rotary phones with durable, hotel-style touchtone models, which blink to let you know somebody's left a message. The television is new, the light fixtures are curved things, modern and brassy. The bathroom sink has a new silver faucet.

I'd come to think of this cabin as a comfortable cage built to contain the me that simmers behind the bourgeois façade I've cultivated to survive academia, with its egos and bullshit and forced civility, where daily my world goes red and my very bones rage and all I want to do is drink, cuss, and throttle people. My cage has changed. Too much, I think.

I pick up the phone and dial zero.

"Front desk," Doyle huffs. His voice makes me want to scratch his throat. "I checked for soap and toilet paper before you got in. Everything should be okay."

"The phones, Doyle. The television! The fixtures!"

"Ain't they nice?"

"I miss a year or two and you go changing the place?"

"Looks mostly, except for the plumbing. County was on me."

"All the cabins?"

"All but mine. I had some money around. Bought that Yahoo! back when, sold it near two hundred. Damn thing split four times."

"You don't own a computer."

"Can't say I do."

"Who's your broker?"

"Reckon I am."

"How'd you know to buy Yahoo!?"

"Some teenagers at the Corbin Best Buy was talking about it—said it was the 'phonebook of the Internet.' Seemed like a good idea to buy me some. Don't everybody use a phone book?"

I stand for a moment with my eyes closed. Then I confess: the market handed me my ass.

"It's a ten-year cycle," he says. "I sell every other time they vote for president. It's like my father used to tell me. 'We don't divide the years into decades, they arrange themselves and divide us.' Only I study they're kind enough to let us figure we're in charge. Best to figure out where you are and sit yourself right."

"Ten-year cycle," I mutter.

"Ye growing an accent?"

"The minute I hit Florence."

"Getting beneath your raisin'."

I look around the room feeling like little bits of civilization and flat-landedness have followed me. I tell him I may be getting below my raising, but he looks like he may be getting a little above his.

Hank calls early. I grumble a greeting.

"You asleep? Awful late, isn't it?"

"I'm on vacation, Hank. Anything the matter?"

"There's an 'out-of-area' on the caller ID. I thought you might have called."

"You? Checking on me? I left a seventeen-year-old boy alone. I should be checking on you. You know where the key to the liquor cabinet is."

"I don't drink. You hungover?"

I sit up and yawn. "What's this about?"

"Nothing."

"Hank." I emphasize his name to let him know my patience is thinning.

"Mom told me what you do down there."

"That's why she's just your mother and not my wife."

"I worry about you."

"I appreciate that."

"Okay if I have Danielle over?"

"I'd be disappointed if you didn't. Make sure you wear—"

"Don't. Please. Please don't say it."

"Why ask? Isn't sneaking half the fun?"

"If you're uptight. We can't go over there."

"Her folks still not sure about you?"

"They're all conservative. I think they vote Republican. Can you believe it? Anyway, it's things like—oh, this—her mom reminding me, like, fifteen times Danielle's grandpa went to Howard for law and was in some big-ass black fraternity where they almost kill you when you pledge."

"I could give her mom a dozen reasons to keep her away from you before I got to your hillbilly family—"

Dial tone.

Doyle comes and we take a walk along Kelly's Branch of the Cumberland. He wants to know more about why I come down here. It's the first time he's asked.

"It's not entirely rational," I say.

"Give old Doyle a try."

"I feel pent up. I come down to be. Has to be here."

"Something in the soil, the water, the Blue Ridge air. It makes folk antsy. Got all that hot blood, living up there everybody wants in your business. The hills call. Bluegrass tickles? You want to get loud. Drink and yell and run around. I know. Believe you me. I don't reckon they take to you—what'd you say you do?"

"Write and teach."

"High school?"

"Community college."

"Don't take to you sipping corn liquor and getting wide with college kids watching." He points to my feet. "You wear them boots to class?"

"I wear work boots to the cabin. Loafers to work."

"Your old lady won't let you out."

"I'm divorced."

"Tomcatting, I figure."

I confess guilt with silence.

"Hot blood, like I said. I bet I know something you don't, professor. We had our own country once. Called it Franklin, after Benjamin. Our only president was Wayne Sevier—he was vain, obstinate, bad tempered, a drunk, an injun killer, whore chaser, and a rotten atheist. Course, he was wildly popular, but the Congress offered to make him governor of Tennessee and he sold the land out from under us. That's right. Got a secret history. You're a citizen of a displaced people. Man without a home, a wanderer wandering—a Palestinian, Kurd, Jew, a Cherokee. Without a patch to call his own a man acts up. Don't know what you're looking for, but you know where to find it. Least you ain't blowed up an airplane."

Doyle tosses his backwash into the poison ivy. He starts back down the path by himself, and I consider the story, which I figure is myth and a load of shit, but which I admire from the gut, nonetheless.

Kelly's Branch is in a dry county, but The El Beau sits just over the county line in downtown Meade, fifteen minutes from Doyle's string of cabins. On weekends, the two-laner between Kelly's Branch and Meade is like bumper cars at the carnival.

Doyle says the fuzz—his word, not mine—set up a roadblock and checkpoint a few years ago, which caused an eight car pile-up when all the drunks tried to drive back to Meade in reverse. Now they let people drive home in peace so long as they're on the right side of the road.

My senses adjust to the smell of sawdust, body odor, and spilled beer. Beer signs in various neon hues blend to a deep red, casting a soft glow on the room that flickers like firelight. The jukebox spins pop country. I motion the bartender over. She has dyed blonde hair, permed wavy, sprayed stiff, and wears a T-shirt advertising an ancient Fort Lauderdale Spring Break. She's damaged and gorgeous.

"What'll it be?"

"What's with the jukebox? This is the El Beau? Where's Hank, Sr.? Bill Monroe?"

"Times change. Liquor ain't sinful enough. We're in competition with oxy. Old-timey music don't help. I gave that jukebox to the Morehead old folks home. You want directions?"

"Give me a draft. Pabst."

I eat some peanuts from a little bowl on the bar. We're alone except for a couple of fat guys who don't look like they've moved in twenty years. One seems to be chewing on something, but I don't think he's really eating anything; the other breathes through his mouth.

"What brings you down?" she asks.

"What makes you think I'm from up north?"

"Looked up Yankee this morning in my Funk & Wagnalls. Your picture, big as life. Now, honey, where you from?"

"Toledo, but my family's from here."

"I got a cousin in Dearborn. Works at the body plant. Bet I know your kin."

"Nash?"

"Hear that, Walt? This old boy here's a Nash."

Walt manages to look both impressed and bored.

"Ain't often seen one in the wild. Thought they was extinct or in captivity."

The other man adjusts his baseball cap and looks me over.

"I used to buy acid off Lienenkugel," he says. "Back before I got saved."

They ask me what I do. I tell them I'm a writer.

"Not your hobby. How you pay your bills?"

There are days when I don't believe writing is much of a career, either. I tell them I'm a teacher, and that seems to satisfy. The bartender tells me her name is Kate and extends her hand. I shake it, telling her I like names that start with a K. They sound strong.

She flexes her biceps, laughs, then jerks Walt another beer. Her jeans are tight enough to be impolite north of the Ohio, but here they seem right, both on her and in the surroundings. Oxys have indeed taken their toll: at midnight, there are still only three of us and Kate.

A few rounds later I start buying shots for the house. First, we do a round of lemon drops, then several bourbons. I unplug the jukebox and start singing bluegrass. They're reluctant at first, but finally Walt and the quiet guy join. Kate closes her stainless steel garnish tray and keeps time on it with her fist.

We run through about six Flatt & Scruggs ditties, and I close with an old song I remember the Old Man singing when I visited Ebb Holler as a boy:

I'm a Saturday nighttime man
But it's a Sunday morning dawning
I'm a Saturday nighttime man
But it's a Sunday morning dawning.

Kate laughs, but I'm ferociously drunk and I don't care. I shout for her to pour another whiskey, rhythm section be damned.

Lord, I paid the devil his due
Lord, I paid him more than you
Lord, the devil took his due
Took me fair 'n square from you
I was hot blooded on my momma's knee
I was hot blooded on my momma's knee
Lord, I was in trouble then
Got a devil down inside of me
I'm a Saturday nighttime man
Lord, I'm a Saturday nighttime man
But it's a Sunday morning dawning
For this Saturday nighttime man.

Kate calls closing, shoos Walter and the quiet man out, locks the door behind them, then tries to help me get straight with putrid coffee in a little blue mug.

"It ain't the cops," she explains. "It's the roads. You'll drive off a cliff."

I pretend to be drunker than I am. I could probably drive.

"If we're waiting on me to sober up, we'll be here all night. Take me home."

She leans over the bar and bats her eyelashes. "Mr. Nash, you're trying to pick me up."

I kiss her and she welcomes my lips. I know then she'll be spending the night. Kate drives my rental car with one hand, with the other she caresses my thighs and face. I kiss her hand and squeeze her breasts through her T-shirt. We clutch each other like teenagers yearning for a place to couple, aching raw. We pull onto the gravel road, passing Doyle's cabin; his bedroom light is on. I wonder what hill magic he's spinning on the world's modern problems. Then Kate squeezes my cock through my pants and for a moment I forget my name.

The little red dome light blinks atop of the phone when we stumble through the door. It crosses my mind to check messages, but Kate's sucking my earlobe. Drunker than I thought, I disrobe sitting on the bed's edge. I'd have been a fool to drive.

Kate pulls her T-shirt over her head and unhooks her bra. Her ample chest and rubbery nipples testify to motherhood, which turns me on. Twenty years ago I'd have had to negotiate my arousal—easy access to birth control led my generation to unplug sex from conception and orgasm from childbirth.

But I watched Debbie unfold, improve, and increase with age. The pressure to bear a child relieved, she felt suddenly released to pursue pleasure for its own sake. Our sex life was never a problem, really, neither before nor after Hank. It was my sex lives with others that caused so much trouble.

With her back to me, Kate hooks her thumbs in her belt loops. In one smooth motion, she lowers her panties and jeans to her ankles. Bent and spread, her buttocks, anus, and pink vulva strike me beautiful and erotic and lewd; I bury my face in her bottom, wrap my arms around her waist and drag her onto the bed.

"You've got your boots on," she says.

I tell her these are the boots I wear for going south.

Kate wakes me with a kiss on the cheek. She lies under my right arm, head on my chest. It's uncomfortable, one of those positions taken by new lovers to expresses affection through little sufferings. I yawn and rub her shoulder.

"I need coffee," she says.

I point at the desk.

"Over there. Say, didn't coffee get you into this fix?"

She pulls back the sheet and rises, as pleasant in the sun as she was under the stars. She strides to the desk naked, shuffles the papers and menus littering the desktop, and lets go a cute little sigh.

"Nothing here."

"Oh, that's right. I brewed it all the other day. Doyle didn't bring more? He's probably up."

"He comes to the bar. He'll look at me funny."

"He will if you don't comb that hair. He's a hospitality provider, Kate. They take discretion seriously."

I start the shower. Before I can step into the tub and pull the curtain closed, she returns, no coffee, and presents a note inscribed in Doyle's wiggly old-man scribble.

Call Hank.

I rearrange the nightstand: lamp upright, shade straight, telephone cord in the jack. The light blinks again, insistent, assertive, and absolute. Kate gathers her clothes.

"I hope everything's okay," she whispers.

I lift the receiver, press nine, and dial home. Morbid scenarios overtake my mind between rings: we got robbed and they hurt my boy. He's done something stupid and gotten arrested. Maybe Danielle's parents went insane and injured him in some dudgeon. A car crash. Debbie? My parents, good

Lord. It crosses my mind to pray, though I don't know what for, or what god would listen. Hank answers on the sixth tone, beating the machine by a ring.

"Nash residence."

"Hank?"

"Where have you been? I've been trying to get hold of you all night. Uncle Wayne, Dad. Uncle Wayne. Uncle Wayne hanged himself. With that rope from papaw's funeral. You know that one he kept? His trophy? They found him yesterday. I'm leaving in a couple hours. You want to meet me in Corbin?"

I open the curtains. It's still early, but daylight takes the window with force and light and sound, stunning me; outside, Doyle walks toward the Cumberland, marking his steps with a carved walking stick. He stops to pick up a plastic bag, then disappears around a bend, swallowed by the chaparral. In a more primitive country, in a more evolved year, he'd be a priest or a senator.

"Dad?"

I put the phone down. Kate sits and rests a soft hand between my shoulder blades. She says I feel cold. I kiss her, soft, on the forehead, and ask her to leave, so I can have some time to think before I pack.

DALE MARLOWE is an author, professor and attorney. He graduated from the Iowa Writers' Workshop in 2002. He lives in Tipp City.